"I'm not going to risk you getting sick on my watch."

A glimpse of the man she'd fallen for all those months ago surfaced. Her nerve endings buzzed with familiarity as Beckett moved on to the next arm and cleaned the rest of the scratches. "There. Less likely you'll die of infection before your next court date."

The physical pain along her forearms ebbed as he secured the gauze and tape over the wounds, but there was an invisible sting behind her sternum. When she'd lost him, Beckett had been just another in the long line of people she couldn't count on sticking around. She'd never known how strong she was until being strong was the only choice she'd had, but right then, a nervous tremor shook her. "Thank you."

"Get some sleep." His voice deepened as though he'd been affected by his action as much as she had, and that, combined with his proximity, hooked into her senses. "Your one chance to prove your innocence starts at dawn."

THE FUGITIVE

NICHOLE SEVERN

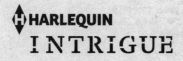

HARLEQUIN
INTRIGUE

This one goes to Becca Syme and her book
Dear Writer, You Need to Quit for convincing me to quit
everything that wouldn't help finish this damn book.

ISBN-13: 978-1-335-40149-6

The Fugitive

Copyright © 2020 by Natascha Jaffa

Recycling programs
for this product may
not exist in your area.

All rights reserved. No part of this book may be used or reproduced in
any manner whatsoever without written permission except in the case of
brief quotations embodied in critical articles and reviews.

This is a work of fiction. Names, characters, places and incidents
are either the product of the author's imagination or are used fictitiously.
Any resemblance to actual persons, living or dead, businesses,
companies, events or locales is entirely coincidental.

This edition published by arrangement with Harlequin Books S.A.

For questions and comments about the quality of this book,
please contact us at CustomerService@Harlequin.com.

Harlequin Enterprises ULC
22 Adelaide St. West, 40th Floor
Toronto, Ontario M5H 4E3, Canada
www.Harlequin.com

Printed in U.S.A.

Nichole Severn writes explosive romantic suspense with strong heroines, heroes who dare challenge them and a hell of a lot of guns. She resides with her very supportive and patient husband, as well as her demon spawn, in Utah. When she's not writing, she's constantly injuring herself running, rock climbing, practicing yoga and snowboarding. She loves hearing from readers through her website, www.nicholesevern.com, and on Twitter, @nicholesevern.

Books by Nichole Severn

Harlequin Intrigue

A Marshal Law Novel

The Fugitive

Blackhawk Security

Rules in Blackmail
Rules in Rescue
Rules in Deceit
Rules in Defiance
Caught in the Crossfire
The Line of Duty

Midnight Abduction

Visit the Author Profile page at Harlequin.com.

CAST OF CHARACTERS

Beckett Foster—This deputy US marshal lives by three words. *Justice. Integrity. Service.* But when his former lover, now a fugitive, charges back into his life, Beckett has to choose between the oath he took to uphold the law and helping the woman with a killer on her trail.

Raleigh Wilde—Falsely charged with fraud and embezzlement, Raleigh is determined more than ever to clear her name for the sake of her unborn baby. Trusting the man who turned his back on her after promising to always be there is a lifeline she can't turn down, but partnering with Beckett is sure to put her life—and her heart—in more danger than ever before.

Hank Foster—Beckett's father was suspected—but never convicted—of stealing thousands of dollars from hardworking Americans as a con man. He's the reason Beckett became a US marshal—and the reason he isn't willing to trust a fugitive.

Finnick Reed—Fellow deputy US marshal assigned out of Beckett's district office. As a former combat medic for the army, Reed is more than capable of having his partner's back.

Remington "Remi" Barton—Chief deputy US marshal and Beckett's superior. She assigned Beckett to recover his fugitive on the promise her marshal wasn't too close to the case, but every step in the investigation has confirmed she shouldn't have taken his word for it.

Chapter One

Raleigh Wilde.

Hell, it'd been a while since deputy United States marshal Beckett Foster had set sights on her, and every cell in his body responded in awareness. Four months, one week and four days, to be exact. Those soul-searching light green eyes, her soft brown hair and sharp cheekbones. But all that beauty didn't take away from the sawed-off shotgun currently pointed at his chest. His hand hovered just above his firearm as the Mothers Come First foundation's former chief financial officer—now fugitive—widened her stance.

"Don't you know breaking into someone's home is illegal, *Marshal*?" That voice. A man could get lost in a voice like that. Sweet and rough all in the same package. Raleigh smoothed her fingers over the gun in her hand. It hadn't taken her but a few seconds after she'd come through the door to realize he'd been waiting for her at the other end of the wide room.

It hadn't taken him but a couple of hours to figure out where she'd been hiding for the past four months once her file crossed his desk. What she didn't know was how long he'd been waiting, and that he'd already relieved that gun of its rounds, as well as any other weapons he'd found during his search of her aunt's cabin.

"Come on now. You and I both know you haven't forgotten my name that easily." He studied her from head to toe, memorizing the fit of her oversize plaid flannel shirt, the slight loss of color in her face and the dark circles under her eyes. Yeah, living on the run did that to a person. Beckett unbuttoned his holster. He wouldn't pull. Of all the criminals the United States Marshals Service had assigned him to recover over the years, she was the only one he'd hesitated chasing down. Then again, if he hadn't accepted the assignment, another marshal would have. And there was no way Beckett would let anyone else bring her in.

Beckett ran his free hand along the exposed brick of the fireplace. "Gotta be honest, didn't think you'd ever come back here. Lot of memories tied up in this place."

"What do you want, Beckett?" The creases around her eyes deepened as she shifted her weight between both feet. She crouched slightly, searching through the single window facing East Lake, then refocused on him.

Looking for a way out? Or to see if he'd come

with backup? Dried grass, changing leaves, mountains and an empty dock were all that were out there. The cabin she'd been raised in as a kid sat on the west side of the lake, away from tourists, away from the main road. Even if he gave her a head start, she wouldn't get far. There was nowhere for her to run. Not from him.

"You know that, too." He took a single step forward, the aged wood floor protesting under his weight as he closed in on her. "You skipped out on your trial, and I'm here to bring you in."

"What was I supposed to do?" Countering his approach, she moved backward toward the front door she'd dead-bolted right after coming inside but kept the gun aimed at him. Her boot hit the go bag she stored on the kitchen counter beside the door. "I didn't steal that money. Someone at the charity did and faked the evidence so I'd take the fall."

"That's the best you got? A frame job?" Fifty and a half million dollars. Gone. The only one with continuous access to the funds stood right in front of him. Not to mention the brand-new offshore bank account, the thousands of wire transfers to that account in increments small enough they wouldn't register for the feds, and Raleigh's signatures on every single one of them. "You had a choice, Raleigh. You just chose wrong."

"Beckett…" She slowed her escape. Her fingers flitted over the gun as her expression softened. "You know me. You know I didn't do this. Find Calvin Dailey, the foundation's CEO. I told him everything when I discovered the funds were being sent offshore. I've been trying to contact him for weeks. He must've gone into hiding when the news about my arrest hit the media, but he can clear my name."

"I'm afraid Calvin Dailey can't help you right now. Seems your boss left his house without about a half a gallon of his own blood. Local police haven't found the body yet, but I don't think that's a coincidence, considering you just revealed he's the only other person you told about the missing money." He locked his jaw against the fire burning through his veins, the easygoing marshal gone. Beckett lowered his hand from above his holster and took another step. "You think you know a person. Then one day you wake up and see them on the morning news getting arrested for embezzlement."

"Calvin's…dead?" Shock dropped her bottom lip. Real dangerous. Either Raleigh Wilde was one hell of an actress, or she honestly hadn't known her former colleague had most likely been murdered. Shock bled to resolution and wiped the confusion from her gaze. She secured the butt of the rifle against her shoulder. Just as he'd taught her. "I didn't kill him, and I didn't embezzle that money. I'm not going to prison. I can't. Not now."

There was the woman he'd let into his life, the one with vengeance in her eyes and her middle fingers raised high. The one who'd stood up to the mugger who'd tried stealing her purse on a Portland street until it'd gotten to the point Beckett had to intervene before she punctured one of the bastard's lungs with her high heel. The one who'd thanked him for his help by intertwining her fingers with his and showing him what real desire looked like. He'd never forget that woman. Too bad she'd never existed in the first place. Instead, he'd gotten involved with a criminal, but she wasn't going to manipulate him again. "That's up to the judge, sweetheart."

"Don't call me that." The words left her mouth between gritted teeth. "You lost the right to call me 'sweetheart' when you disappeared after my arrest."

"And here I was thinking you're the one who broke us up." He pulled a set of cuffs from the back of his holster, shards of reflected sunlight bouncing across her face. "I'm bringing you in."

"I'll give you one chance to walk away, Beckett." She racked the shotgun, her expression softening slightly. "Please. For both our sakes, don't make me pull this trigger. Turn around and pretend you never found me. It's better for everyone if I stay lost."

"You're going to shoot me now, is that it?" It was possible. Honestly, how well did he really know her? They'd been together six months before she'd gotten arrested. Sure, she'd let her past slip out every once in a while, but, it turned out, nearly everything he'd known about her had been a lie. The deeper he'd dug into her life, the more he'd realized how stupid he'd been to trust her. People didn't change. Once a criminal, always a criminal.

"I'll do whatever it takes to survive." The shadows across her throat shifted as she licked her lips and swallowed. "This isn't just about me anymore."

Beckett stuck his hand in his jeans pocket and pulled out the rounds he'd taken from the gun. Pinching one between his thumb and index finger, he held it up for her to see. "How are you going to shoot me if the gun is empty, Raleigh?"

She faltered, her green gaze lowering to the weapon.

Beckett dropped the cuffs and the rounds and lunged. Ripping the rifle from her grip with one hand, he unholstered his own weapon and aimed with the other. In less than two breaths, he had his fugitive. The shotgun hit the floor, jarring her instantly. Nice to see there were still some things that could get through that carefully monitored exterior. "Now I can guarantee you this gun is loaded." He motioned her to the left with the barrel of his service weapon. "Cuffs. Now."

"You're making a mistake. If Calvin was killed as you said, whoever stole that money is cleaning up loose ends. He's the only one I told about the missing money. Who do you think they'll come after next?" Raleigh crouched, picked up the handcuffs and secured one over her wrist. The cords between her shoulders and neck flexed tight as she moved. She straightened, facing him, her light vanilla scent making its way deep into his lungs. "You take me in, you'll only make it easier for his killer to find me."

He ensured the cuffs were tight enough she couldn't squirm loose, his fingers brushing the inside of her wrist. An electric jolt shot up his arm in response. Hell. He'd forgotten what it was like to touch her, how his body had always craved hers. His heart threatened to beat out of his chest, his lungs pressurizing with the air stuck in his throat. Six months. That'd been all the time he'd needed to fall for her, she'd been that addictive. He'd run to help when some purse snatcher had tried to take off with her bag, but, in reality, she'd been the one to save him that day. She'd changed…everything, given him hope he didn't have to spend the rest of his life alone. Until he'd learned who she really was. Learned it'd all been one long con.

The cuffs ratcheted into place, the clicks loud in his ears as he secured her hands in front, and reality bled into focus. Justice. Integrity. Service. He'd sworn to uphold the law when he'd become a marshal, and the woman in front of him wouldn't change that. No matter how strong her gravitational pull. Or how clever her lies. "No, Raleigh. The mistake was trusting you from the beginning."

"I'm not going back." She stared out the window over his shoulder, almost lost, green eyes ethereal. Seconds ticked by. Then, in an instant, her gaze snapped back to his, and his instincts screamed in warning. Raleigh wrenched away from him, then kicked him square in the gut. "Not until I clear my name."

His head hit the old wood mantel above the fireplace—hard—and he went down. The cabin blurred in his vision as he struggled to his feet; the only illumination came from a beam of sunlight through the now open front door. It was enough to give him direction. The go bag from the kitchen counter was gone. He pressed his free hand to the back of his head, then glanced at his fingers. Blood. Pain spread fast through his skull. Damn, that woman had powerful legs. Beckett charged out the door, gun up, finger on the trigger. He blinked against the brightness glinting off the lake and shook his head to clear the soft ringing in his ears. "Raleigh!"

Movement registered along the lake's shore about fifty feet to his left. Cuffed, she sprinted toward a thick line of trees behind the cabin, all that soft brown hair trailing behind her.

Beckett pumped his legs hard. The sun had already started hugging the mountains. If she evaded him long enough, there was a chance she'd disappear forever. That wasn't an option. Raleigh vanished into the tree line ahead of him. Loose rocks and fallen branches threatened to trip him up, but he only pushed himself harder.

His heart thundered behind his ears as shadows enveloped the small dirt trail ahead. Too many damn places for an ambush. He slowed, sweat beading in his hairline, and forced the adrenaline pumping through his veins to cool. His training kicked in, instincts on high alert. Raleigh might be a criminal, but she wasn't a trained law-enforcement officer. Any family she'd ever had had turned their backs on her a long time ago, and her friends had been advised to keep their distance by counsel. She couldn't hide from him. At least, not for long.

The sound of a broken twig snapping in two twisted him to the right. He took aim as branches of a fir tree swayed with the fresh breeze. Tension tightened every muscle down his spine. Three seconds. Four. A shadow slipped into his peripheral vision off to the left, and he spun, too late.

Thick dried bark scraped across the exposed skin of his arm a split second before he ducked out of the way of the massive branch she'd swung at him. He lunged as she widened her stance for another round, hiking her over his shoulder in a fireman's hold. A sharp jab of her knee knocked the air from his lungs. A growl rumbled through his chest as they hit the forest floor. He pinned her beneath him, all that lean muscle and soft skin. "You're making this harder on yourself."

Raleigh hooked her foot under his shin and shoved, trying to roll him onto his back. Wouldn't work. Struggling for purchase, she bucked her hips up to dislodge his advantage. Fire ignited the subtle hints of gold around the edges of her eyes.

He secured her wrists between his hands and pulled her to her feet. "You're under arrest."

HEARTS WERE WILD CREATURES. Traitorous, deceitful creatures who didn't know the difference between the US marshal who intended on bringing her in and the man she'd envisioned spending the rest of her life with up until a few months ago.

Raleigh Wilde focused on where her boots landed along the trail and not on the fact she'd actually been happy to see him. Those coastal-blue eyes, his thick dark hair she used to tangle her fingers through or his beard that would tickle her throat when he kissed her. Not to mention every ridge and valley of muscle she'd memorized from the first day they'd met all those years ago.

It'd been four months since the last time they'd stood face-to-face, and this was how it was going to end? Beckett would bring her into the Marshals' district office, turn her over to the FBI, and whoever'd framed her for taking that donation money would enjoy their freedom while she served time for a crime she didn't commit. Because, of all the things she hadn't been able to depend on in this world, Beckett and his unbreakable sense of duty was something she could count on.

She sucked in a lungful of clean Oregon air. Dried needles crunched beneath her feet, red, orange and yellow foliage clinging to the thick line of trees around her aunt's small property. It'd been a long time since she'd had the guts to come back out here. Not since her brother's death. Pressing her cuffed wrists against her lower abdomen, she shook her head. She should've known Beckett Foster would be assigned her case. He was the one who knew her best, after all. The only one she'd trusted with pieces of herself. He'd known she'd come here. But she wasn't a criminal. No matter what he believed about her or what the evidence said. She hadn't stolen a dime from the foundation she and Calvin had built together, and she'd prove it. She'd clear her name and get her life back. She slid the edge of her thumb over the growing baby bump she kept hidden. Get her future back. "I never meant for you to get involved in any of this."

"Don't talk to me like we're friends." His heavy steps echoed loud behind her. The sun had gone down behind the mountains, making the dangerous tone in his voice that much more terrifying. The slide of steel against her spine kept her moving. Twenty feet, maybe less, until they left the safety of the trees. "My head is still bleeding."

She was out of time. She couldn't go to prison. She could run again, but he was so much stronger than she was, faster, bigger. Raleigh slowed. His dark, rich scent still lodged in her lungs. Outdoors and man. She hadn't realized how much she'd missed that comforting smell until just now. She dug her nails into her palms against the truth. She hadn't realized how much she'd missed him. They were nearing the edge of the tree line. He'd parked his truck straight ahead. The second he put her in that vehicle, it was over. She had to tell him the truth. She had to make him believe her. "Beckett, there's something I have to tell—"

A gunshot exploded from the trailhead, echoing off the mountains at their back.

Fire burned along the edge of her neck as strong hands ripped her off the trail and into the trees. In the span of a single breath, Beckett shoved them behind a large fir. Protecting her? Raleigh clamped a hand over the wound as he drew his weapon.

Beckett released the magazine from the gun, checked it, then slammed it back into place. Just as he'd taught her when he'd insisted she needed to learn how to handle a weapon. He spun, facing her. Rough calluses tugged at her skin as he forced her hand out of the way and studied her wound. "How bad is it?"

Her heart jerked behind her rib cage as his fingers brushed against the oversensitized skin of her throat. That almost sounded like concern in his voice. But she knew better. He'd protect her because she was a fugitive whose file had come across his desk. He'd get her back into federal custody, even if he had to shoot his way out of here to do it. She was a job. Nothing more. Anything they had together had been destroyed the moment he'd turned his back on her after her arrest. Bright blue eyes locked on her, and her blood heated in an instant. She hissed as the salt in his skin aggravated the bullet's burn on her neck and pulled back. "It's a graze. I'm fine."

"Good." Beckett turned his back to her, all that concern that'd warmed her from the inside turning to ice. "Then you know the drill. Stay behind me, and don't even think about running again."

"Exactly where am I supposed to go?" she asked.

A short burst of laughter shook his shoulders. "Didn't stop you from trying a few minutes ago."

Another bullet ripped through the tree at her right, and she flinched away as fear took control. Her fingers tightened in his shirt, the cuffs cutting into the soft tissue of her inner wrists. They had to get out of here. Raleigh patted him on the shoulder. "Where are your handcuff keys?"

"US Marshals Service! Put your weapon down, get on your knees and put your hands behind your head!" Beckett pulled the trigger. Once. Twice. The shadow disappeared from the edge of the trees, but Raleigh wasn't naive enough to believe the shooter had suddenly grown a conscience and backed down. Calvin's disappearance couldn't be coincidence, and neither was the fact someone had come for her minutes after Beckett showed up. He'd been followed. And he'd led a killer straight to her. "The cuffs stay on. You're not getting away from me again."

She focused on the slight bulge beneath his lower pant leg. Screw the cuffs. She wasn't going to die out here. She had too much to lose. Hiking up Beckett's

pant leg, she unholstered the small revolver he kept
strapped to his ankle and fired three shots toward
the shooter.

Beckett twisted around. "What the hell are you
doing?"

"Giving us a fighting chance." She left the cover
of trees along the trail, positioning herself as a
smaller target, and backed farther into the woods.
They'd have to find another way out. Whoever'd
shot at them had them pinned down, and they knew
it. If Beckett wanted to get her into federal custody,
he'd have to do things her way. "I know these woods
better than anyone. If you want to get out of here
alive, you'll do exactly as I say. Unless your oversize ego won't let me save your life."

He stepped out from behind the massive fir he'd
shoved her behind when the bullets had started flying, gun raised at the entrance to the trail. "I don't
trust criminals."

Air lodged in her lungs. Was that what this was
all about? Why he hadn't come to see her in county
lockup. Why he hadn't returned her dozens of calls
once she'd been arrested. She'd taken a risk revealing the pieces of her past she'd shared with him,
her need to have someone to rely on when so many
others—family, friends—had up and disappeared
from her life. She'd trusted him, believed the promise he'd made to stick by her side, no matter what
happened. But, in the end, he'd been exactly like the
rest of them. Unreliable. Self-righteous.

Her heart thundered in her chest as she studied his broad shoulders. She didn't have to see those light eyes to sense the disgust surging through him, and her stomach twisted with nausea. He'd spent over a decade chasing fugitives for the Marshals Service, experiencing firsthand how evil people could be. She sucked in a shaky breath. Was that how he saw her now? As one of the bad guys?

Four more rounds exploded through the trees and hurled her back into the moment. Raleigh returned fire until the gun clicked empty. She tossed his backup weapon. Wouldn't do them a damn bit of good in these woods. She'd stashed go bags all over this mountainside, including the one she'd hidden a few yards away. Except there was no extra ammunition for Beckett's revolver. She drowned the hurt that'd been bottling inside for the hundredth time and pulled him deeper off the trail. "I don't think you have a choice."

Needles and leaves scratched at her skin as they ran into the trees. Another gunshot rang loud in her ears but arced wide. The sun had set behind the mountain. There was no way their attacker could spot them now, but hiking through the woods in the middle of the night brought on its own set of problems. She had to get to the first supply bag she'd buried before the shooter caught up with them.

No pressure.

Beckett's strong grip wrapped around her arm and pulled her into his chest. She planted the sides of her hands above his heart for balance, and heat surged into her neck and face at the contact. Hard muscle shifted beneath her fingers, his breath light on her skin, and suddenly the weeks—months— since she'd last touched him disappeared. "You're not going anywhere."

"I'm sorry—I thought we were concerned about the gunman shooting at us." Only the outline of his shadow and the feel of his heartbeat beneath her palm registered in the darkness. Too close. Too real. Too painful. The small life growing inside her flut- tered, and it took every ounce of strength she had not to smooth her palm over her stomach in assur- ance. Raleigh pressed away and wrenched out of his grip. "We need to keep moving."

A small click preceded the beam of a flashlight from behind, but she kept pushing one foot in front of the other. He'd come prepared with a flashlight. Always the Boy Scout. "Whatever you're planning, it won't work."

She slowed, the weight of his attention, even in the dark, a physical pressure along her spine. Insects quieted, a light breeze rustling the dead foliage at her feet. Temperatures had already started to drop, but the emotional pain she'd ignored earlier bubbled to the surface. "All I'm planning to do, Beckett, is survive." She faced him, raising her hands against the brightness of the flashlight. "Because in case you've forgotten, the only person I told about the missing donation funds is presumably dead, and someone just tried to shoot us."

"I'm supposed to believe those two situations are linked? Hell, for all I know, that could've been an accomplice getting even when you took off with the money." He lowered the flashlight to his side, his weapon still unholstered. Would he shoot her? After everything they'd been through, had her arrest really brought her so low in his eyes? "You're one of the most intelligent women I've come across, Raleigh. You could've set up this entire charade to insert yourself back in my life, planning to get a US marshal on your side of things, but it won't work. You and I are done. Pretending you're in danger isn't going to change that."

Guess that answered her question. He'd made up his mind about their future the moment Portland Police Bureau had put the cuffs on her, and there was nothing she could do to change it. Fine. Raleigh swallowed the rejection charging up her throat and leveled her chin with the ground. He wanted the truth? She'd give him more truth than he could handle. "I'm pregnant, Beckett. With your baby."

"What?" The flashlight beam shook in his hand, his voice barely audible over the breeze sweeping through the woods.

"You can accuse me of whatever you want. Embezzlement, orchestrating Calvin's death, planning some elaborate scenario in which I play the damsel in distress to get your protection. I don't care." Lie.

What they'd had… It wasn't supposed to be like this. Raleigh rolled her shoulders back, then closed in on him, the fury tearing through her uncontrollable. "The only thing that matters to me is clearing my name so I can give this baby the life they deserve."

He didn't answer. Didn't even move.

She turned her back on him, forcing herself deeper into the forest. "And I'm not going to let you stop me."

Chapter Two

Impossible. It was another manipulation, a poison meant to get into his head and force him to reconsider his assignment. He'd learned fairly young to spot a con a mile off, thanks to his father. Raleigh's attempt to get him to sympathize wouldn't play out like she wanted. They'd been intimate, sure, but they'd been careful—each and every time. "I think you'll say just about anything to keep from paying for what you've done, to not answer for how many people you hurt."

Her retreat slowed up ahead, until she stopped cold. She lowered the back of her head onto her shoulders. Almost in defeat, but Beckett knew better. He knew her, and there wasn't a single bone in this woman's all-too-familiar body that would accept failure. She'd helped build an entire foundation from the ground up dedicated to lowering pregnancy mortality rates throughout the world. She was driven, ambitious and had her eyes on only one goal the entire time they'd been together: to succeed.

She faced him, that mesmerizing gaze meeting his in the dim beam from his flashlight, and right then, he could only kick himself for underestimating her in the first place. He should've known better than to fall for the victim play all those months ago, but if there was one thing he hated more than the criminals who thought they were above the law, it was finding out about the people they hurt along the way. He wouldn't let her or any one of them get away with breaking the law. No matter how much the hollowness in his chest wanted her claims to be true, wanted what they'd had to be true, she wasn't who he'd believed. Raleigh took a step toward him, then another.

He'd cuffed her wrists in front of her, but that didn't detract from the gut-wrenching sway of her hips as she closed the distance between them. Mere inches separated them when she stopped, every cell in his body in tune to her slightest movement, the smallest change in her expression. Just as he'd always been. "Left back pocket."

"Your confession in there? Because that's the only thing I'm interested in." Annoyance deepened the distinct lines between her brows, and he couldn't help but revel in the fact he'd managed to break through that curated exterior.

"Yeah. I carry it around in case you were the one assigned to arrest me and drag me back to the feds." The cuffs rattled as Raleigh rubbed her thumb beneath the metal. Crystallized puffs of air formed in front of that perfect mouth of hers as the temperature dropped, but he wouldn't feel the least bit sorry she hadn't thought to grab a coat when she'd tried to outrun him. She stepped into him. "You want to know what I think?"

Four months should've been enough to shut down the automatic spike in his blood pressure when she got this close, and that reaction left him more unbalanced than he wanted to admit. "Not really."

"I think you're so set on making me the enemy, Beckett, you've blinded yourself to anything that might prove I'm innocent." She maneuvered her wrists to one side and dug deep into the back left pocket of her jeans. Her flannel shirt contoured to the shape of her body in the dim light, and for a second, he could've sworn there was a slight curve around the front of her hips that hadn't been there before. She pulled a piece of folded paper free, setting it against his chest with both hands before shoving away from him. "Is that the kind of marshal you really want to be?"

The accusation hit exactly where she'd intended and threatened to knock him back on his heels. He slid his hand over the thin, glossy paper as she turned away from him and hiked back up the small rise. Deviating course to a large tree off to the right, she collapsed to her knees and used both hands to start digging at the base, but Beckett couldn't move. Couldn't think.

After everything she'd done, she had the guts

to question his integrity? He'd spent the past decade chasing down the worst this country had to offer, fugitives exactly like her, in an effort to prove the tree he'd fallen from hadn't corrupted his core. Suspects lied to him on a daily basis, ran to keep him from uncovering their secrets and played mind games any chance they got to convince him he had the wrong guy. He wasn't blind. He saw them for exactly what they were, and no amount of manipulation from Raleigh or anyone else would change his outlook as long as he wore this badge. One way or another, he was bringing her in to answer for her crimes. Just as Beckett's father would answer for his when he caught up with him.

Gravity seemed to increase its effect on his shoulders as he unfolded the black-and-white photo. Air stuck halfway up his throat. He studied the gray blurred shape against the dark background under the flashlight beam, could almost count the individual fingers on one hand of the fetus lying horizontally across the sonogram. No. This wasn't... Couldn't be.

His heart beat hard at the base of his throat as she sauntered back toward him. A dark backpack hung from her grip in his peripheral vision, but he couldn't take his attention off the delicate paper photo in his hand. Raleigh's name, the date and time were stamped in the upper right-hand corner, below that the name of the OB-GYN practice that'd provided the ultrasound. Twenty weeks, a little over five months. She might not have known she was pregnant when she'd been arrested, but now the truth was clearer than ever. Along with the arrow pointing directly at three small white lines between the baby's legs. His gut jerked. "You're having a girl."

"*We're* having a girl." She slid dirt-stained fingers over his wrist.

Heat exploded through him at the contact. His fingers ached to crumple the sonogram in his hand, but he forced himself to breathe evenly, to think this through. She was pregnant, with his child, but that didn't mean a damn in the eyes of the law. His stomach soured. Now they were tied together for life. He held up the sonogram between his index and middle fingers. "What exactly was the plan here? Show me this and I'd suddenly want to use my Marshal status to prove you're not the one who took that money? You keep this on you in case I was the one assigned to your recovery?"

"I don't… What do you mean?" Shock smoothed her expression, her mouth parting. Hell, she was good. Perfect at playing any role she needed to get under his skin. Those compelling green eyes narrowed on him, and somehow a shiver settled under his skin as though she'd physically touched him. Raleigh snatched the sonogram from him, the pack she carried in her other hand dragging her cuffed wrists in front of her. The tendons between her neck and shoulders flexed as she stepped away. "You think me getting pregnant was planned? That I had an ulterior motive to keep you in my life in case I was charged with fraud and embezzlement?"

"It's amazing how far criminals will go out of their way to prove they're innocent," he said.

The sun had already gone down. Cold worked under his clothing, his fingers aching against the metal of his flashlight. They'd have to camp here tonight. No point in getting themselves lost in the middle of the woods when the shooter was still out there. "We'll rest here tonight. Give me your hands."

"I'm not a criminal." Her tone almost sounded as though she'd convinced herself as she offered her wrists.

Instant sensation of familiarity arched through him. Leading her to the nearest tree small enough to get her arms wrapped around, Beckett unpocketed the handcuff key and released one of the cuffs, then wound her arms around the tree. The cuff clicked back into place. "Tell that to your aunt, Raleigh."

Her hold on that legendary control slipped. Her eyes widened, her sharp inhalation cutting through the silence around them.

"You didn't think I'd find out about that, did you? I have to admit, it took me calling in a lot of favors to have those records unsealed, but in the end—" he turned to collect the pack she'd dug out of the ground, then faced her "—I know exactly who you are, Raleigh Wilde. You're a killer, a thief, and there's nothing you can do or say to convince me you're not exactly like the rest of the fugitives I'm assigned to hunt. Guilty."

"Then I guess there's nothing left for us to talk about, is there?" she asked.

How he'd been so blinded during the time they'd been together he had to attribute to the fact she'd done everything she could to hide her past from him. And she'd done a damn fine job. She'd fooled him and everyone else around her. He should've known the whirlwind romance he'd instantly been sucked into had only been the first step of her plan. Now she'd ensured he wouldn't be able to walk away after turning her over to the feds. Not with her pregnant with his baby.

Unzipping her pack, he emptied its contents onto the ground and riffled through them. A change of clothes, a tarp, flashlight with additional batteries, matches, packages of food and a couple of water bottles. Enough to last them a day, maybe a day and a half if they rationed their supplies. And a Glock 22, most likely from the collection of weapons he'd found in her aunt's cabin. He released the magazine and pocketed it, clearing the chamber before wedging it between his jeans and lower back.

"What's your plan, Marshal?" Shifting, she tried to put space between her and the tree bark grating against her oversize shirt. In vain. He wasn't giving her a chance to run this time. His head still hurt from the last time she'd caught him by surprise. "Hide out here until the gunman who tried to kill us loses interest, then just walk me through the Marshals' office front doors?"

"If that gets your file off my desk and you serve your time." Beckett collected a few dead twigs and dry grass from another grouping of trees, arranged a circle of rocks around a small cone shape he'd made with the kindling, then used one of the matches from her pack to light the fire. Snow hadn't started falling this late in the year yet, but there was a frosty bite in the air Beckett couldn't chase from his veins. Whether it came from the dropping temperatures or from the woman currently handcuffed to the tree a few feet away, he had no idea. Didn't want to know. "Win-win."

"If you take me back, I'll spend at least the next five years in prison for something I didn't do." Her voice shook. "Is that what you want for your daughter? Our daughter?"

Beckett raised his gaze to hers over the fire he'd lit between them, then stood. No. It wasn't. There were plenty of kids who turned out just fine after learning the people who were supposed to care about them were monsters, but he hadn't been one of them. He'd spent his entire life trying to make up for what his father had done, and there was no way in hell he'd put any kid of his through that same pain. Rounding the perimeter of rocks he'd used to create a barrier around the campfire, he checked the cuffs at her wrists. The sonogram was still clutched in her fist, and his gut clenched. "All right, Raleigh.

You say you're innocent? I'll give you one chance to prove it before I drag you back to the feds." He leveled his voice to convince himself he didn't feel anything for her or their situation, anything at all. "But if you're lying to me, I'll make sure you never see that baby again."

RAIN PATTERED LIGHTLY on her shoulder, cut through her hair straight to her scalp. A tremor rocked through her, then another. The fire held on, warming her boots and toes, but even with the exhaustion pulling at her muscles, Raleigh couldn't sleep. Beckett had given his word he'd let her prove she hadn't stolen the funds from Mothers Come First—her foundation—but he'd made promises before.

And broken every single one.

She'd watched countless mothers across the globe receive the help they needed and deserved because of the foundation. Prenatal care, postpartum services, sex education, ambulance services to rural areas. The work she'd dedicated her entire adult life to achieving made a difference. It'd saved lives. If there'd been an organization like hers when she and her brother had been born, maybe their mother would've survived the blood clot that'd killed her two days after childbirth. Maybe their lives would've turned out differently. Maybe her brother would still be alive.

Who would want to destroy that by stealing millions of dollars in donations? Who would try to have her killed to keep her from uncovering the truth? And how could Beckett think she'd had anything to do with it?

Raleigh shifted against the tree he'd cuffed her to, rubbing at the rawness between the metal and skin. She'd gotten into the habit of sliding her hands over her growing belly when she needed assurance, but with the cuffs, she was resigned to studying the man who'd put them on in the first place. The man who saw her as nothing more than a fugitive.

Beckett hadn't changed much over the past few months. Thick dark beard around his jaw, matching hair she'd run her fingers through a hundred times. Rain contoured thick cords of muscle along his chest and thighs as his clothing suctioned to his body, and an answering heat to all his contained power ignited deep inside. The lines around the blue eyes she hadn't been able to get out of her head had gotten deeper. There was a hardness in his expression that hadn't been there before, but under all the bitterness and the invisible wall he'd built between them, he was still the same man who'd come to her aid in the middle of that Portland street less than a year ago. Still committed, defensive and cautious as ever.

"Stop staring at me." That all-too-familiar voice warmed areas where dropping temperatures left her defenseless, and her throat dried. Which didn't make sense. He'd hurt her, more than anyone had before, but her heart hadn't gotten the damn idea.

She'd trusted him to keep his word, to always be there when she needed him. Then he'd disappeared the moment news of her arrest went public. Beckett Foster didn't deserve anything from her, and she sure as hell wasn't going to give him the satisfaction of coming quietly.

Keeping the brim of his hat low over his eyes, he shifted against the tree where he'd taken up guard duty, the butt of his weapon visible from here. He intertwined his fingers below his sternum and crossed his boots at the ankles, perfectly at ease out here in the wild. "If you're waiting for me to fall asleep so you can make another run for it, don't bother."

"You're a light sleeper. I remember." He'd taken the supplies from the pack she'd buried in case she'd needed a quick escape and stripped down her weapon. While she had more packs buried out here, he held on to her only weapon. But she wasn't going anywhere. For now. The last of the fire smoked out as the storm thundered overhead. Her clothes had soaked through in a matter of minutes. A shiver chased down her spine, the major muscles in her legs tightening against the cold. They couldn't go back to the cabin. Not with a gunman hunting them through these woods, but there was a chance she'd freeze to death out here before Beckett could turn her over to the feds.

Pressure built behind her breastbone, and she raised her gaze to meet his. Instant awareness charged every nerve she owned, as though she'd laid eyes on him for the first time. His lips parted on a strong exhalation as he sat up and reached for the tarp beside him. In a matter of erratic heartbeats, he stood over her. Water clung to the sharp angles of his face as he arranged the edges of the tarp overhead so she was protected from the downpour. "You should've brought a coat. Won't do either of us any good if you drop into hypothermia."

"I was more concerned about outrunning you than fashion at the time." She licked the water from her mouth, and his gaze homed in on the action, sending a rush of lightness straight through her. The lack of rain sliding down her scalp and into her collar was already helping her warm up, but her hands still shook. The cuffs rattled around the tree, her jaw aching against the chattering of her teeth. She couldn't feel her fingers, and her toes had started going numb without the warmth of the fire.

He maneuvered under the tarp, taking the handcuff keys from his back pocket in the same move. Strong fingers slid around her arm as Beckett twisted the key and pried the cuffs from around her wrists.

She pulled both hands in to her chest. Red-and-pink scratches puckered down the length of the thin skin of her forearms from the tree bark, but while the physical pain hurt, the bruising in her heart ached more. Crossing her arms over her midsection, she leaned into the tops of her thighs. "Thanks."

"It's one thing not to trust you—it's another to

watch you freeze to death on my watch." He sat beside her, muscled arms brushing against her side.

Right. Because this was just another fugitive-recovery assignment for him. When—if—they were able to prove she'd been framed for taking all that money, he still had to bring her in for skipping out on her trial. Best-case scenario, the truth would come out, the charges would be dropped and they'd each move on with their lives. That was the job, and the knot in her stomach constricted as loss tore through her.

The neutrality smoothing his expression didn't show any evidence of the thoughts running through his head. He'd cut her off from the man she'd known, cut her out of his life faster than most people took to rip off a Band-Aid, and there wasn't a single moment out here on the run when she'd forgotten that choice. She'd known the risk of letting someone close again, known the people she'd cared for the most would have the power to cause the most damage, but she'd been willing to take that risk. For him. Raleigh hugged her knees, the waistband of her jeans fitting tighter than a few weeks ago. Only now she wasn't the only one who'd end up paying the price. "Beckett, I know this situation isn't ideal—"

"Let's get one thing straight. I'm giving you one chance to prove your innocence solely because you claim that baby you've got in there is mine. Anything else is off the table, understand?" He dug his heels into the mud, rain echoing off the tarp overhead, and she bit back the apology at the tip of her tongue. He kept his gaze ahead, on some distant point instead of her, and she nodded. She understood. He was doing this for their unborn child, not her, and if he could have it his way, he would've chosen someone—anyone—else to take on that calling. "You're the CFO of the foundation. There can't be that many people aside from you with access to the donations account. If you're not the one who embezzled it, as you say, then tell me who else could get their hands on that money without raising any red flags."

Raleigh forced herself to take a deep breath as the sickening twist in her stomach intensified. She'd helped found Mothers Come First, had vetted nearly every employee herself. Even after all these months, it was still hard to imagine any of them had stolen from the charity, but she'd mapped out her own suspect list soon after escaping federal custody. "The foundation employs thirteen accountants in Finance and Fund Services. There's Calvin Dailey, the CEO, but…" Bile worked up her throat. But according to Beckett, her founding partner had been killed in his own home. She felt light-headed as reality hit. Calvin would've been the only one who could've cleared her name. She cleared her throat, focusing her attention on the scratches carved into her forearms from the tree bark. Her shirt should've been enough to protect her from the bark while she'd been cuffed, but it'd ridden up when she'd tried picking the lock. At the time, the pain had been worth it. Now, not so much. "Then we have two fund services accountants who oversee the daily donations coming in and the money going out. Plus, my assistant, Emily."

"Then we'll start there." His gaze dipped to her arms, the weight of those hypnotic blue eyes hiking her heart rate into overdrive. Before she had a chance to take her next breath, he reached for her. Rough calluses caught against her skin as he unfolded her arms away from her midsection and smoothed his thumb across the small, angry lacerations. "We're going to have to clean those before they get infected."

"I'm fine." She tugged at her wrist as the hollowness in her chest flared, but he only tightened his hold on her. Blood rushed to the oversensitized skin along her arms.

"I'm not going to risk you getting sick on my watch." Keeping her arm in his grip, he dug into her go bag with his free hand and pulled the small first-aid kit from the depths. In seconds, the antiseptic burn spread across her skin as Beckett brushed the alcohol pad down along the tendons of her forearms and left a relieving coolness in its wake. Dirt lined the edges of his fingernails, that signature scent of wood and earth filling her senses, and a glimpse of the man she'd fallen for all those months ago surfaced. The one who'd put himself at risk to fight off a mugger on her behalf, however unnecessary it'd been at the time. Who'd ensured she'd gotten home safely and bandaged the wound in her palm when she'd cut her hand on the sidewalk after the attack. Her nerve endings buzzed with familiarity as Beckett moved on to the next arm and cleaned the rest of the scratches. "There. Less likely you'll die of infection before your next court date."

The physical pain along her forearms ebbed as he secured gauze and tape over the wounds, but there was an invisible sting in her chest. She'd been fine on her own, taken care of herself for as long as she remembered. Losing her mother right after childbirth, never knowing her father. Then having her brother taken from her right in front of her eyes when she'd been fifteen. Losing Beckett had just been another in the long line of people she couldn't count on sticking around. She'd never known how strong she was until being strong was the only choice she'd had, but right now, a nervous tremor shook through her. "Thank you."

"Get some sleep." His voice deepened as though he'd been affected by his action as much as she had, and that, combined with his proximity, hooked into her senses. "Your one chance to prove your innocence starts at dawn."

Chapter Three

He could still feel her, feel the softness of her skin against the calluses on his fingers. What the hell had he been thinking, playing nurse like that? As far as he was concerned, Raleigh Wilde was exactly what the prosecuting attorney believed, the very thing he'd battled to stop his entire career. A fugitive. Here he was, cleaning her wounds like what she'd done didn't matter.

Her head rested against his arm, the slow rise and fall of her chest telling him she'd finally fallen asleep, but he couldn't move. He could hardly breathe, and he definitely couldn't think. Long, damp hair plastered to the angles of her familiar jawline, and his fingers tingled to sweep it back behind her ear. Rain lightened against the tarp above them. That, along with their combined body heat, had chased back the numbness in his fingers and toes, but it'd take a lot more than her word to break through the caution he'd relied on to keep himself alive. Beckett curled his hands into fists. One minute, she'd been everything to him, and in cuffs the next.

Now a shooter had tried to kill her, one he highly doubted she'd hired herself. Hell, he could admit it'd been one of his weakest moments considering the idea, because despite the proof stacked against her, Raleigh had gotten one thing right. He hadn't been willing to see evidence she might be innocent. Not after she'd run from him.

The past rushed to meet the present, and Beckett squeezed his eyes shut. His mother's scream echoed in his head. Over and over. There'd been a gun, blood. Fear. He hadn't been able to stop any of it. His father had stolen millions of dollars from hard-working Americans, and one of those Americans had broken into their family home to make him pay. Only the gunman hadn't found his father that night. The bastard had taken off a few months before. No warning. No note. Just up and left Beckett and his mother to fend for themselves on the ranch passed down from his maternal grandparents. Instead of finding revenge, with a single pull of a trigger, the man who'd lost everything to Hank Foster had taken away the only parent Beckett had left when he'd been sixteen. It'd all been his father's fault.

"Hey." That sweet voice, the one that'd haunted him the last four months, broke through his defenses as her hand slid across his chest. Stinging heat exploded through his system as his heart rate tried to keep up with his shallow breathing. Raleigh rubbed soothing circles over the left side of his chest, her voice soft as reality bled into focus. "Are you okay?"

Red and oranges crept across the sky and damp earth of the clearing they'd camped in for the night. Damn it, he must've fallen asleep. Beckett scrubbed his face and beard with one hand, his defenses growing stronger second by slow, agonizing second. "I'm fine."

"You still have nightmares." Not a question, but he couldn't help but tense all the same. There'd been times when he'd woken in a cold sweat from the memories of that night, but having her pressed against him, her rubbing his back in soothing circles the same way she was doing now, had made the transition back to sleep easier. He'd spent years training to become a lawman, ready to balance out the hurt and pain Hank Foster had caused by bringing criminals like his father to justice, but in those moments with her, Beckett had felt safe. Supported. Something he hadn't felt in a long time.

"It's nothing." He brushed her hand from his chest and shoved to his feet. He ripped the tarp out of his way. The smell of cleansing rain, earth and wet wood penetrated his senses, but none of it was strong enough to dislodge her vanilla scent from his lungs. Beckett forced himself to clear his head, to focus. She had a federal warrant out for her arrest and a gunman on her trail. They'd wasted enough time. Because the sooner he proved Raleigh was exactly what he thought her to be, the sooner he could move on with his life—for good. "We need to keep moving."

"You've been having them for years, and that's all you say when I ask. That it's nothing." She got to her feet, those all-too-familiar green eyes searching his expression, but she wouldn't get anything. Not from him. Had they stayed together, there might've been a point where he'd trusted her with the truth, but that day was long past. She'd made sure of that. "I was there, Beckett. In the middle of the night, when you were screaming and shaking. I was the one who helped you get back to sleep, who reminded you that you were safe."

This conversation wasn't happening. "I never asked you to do that."

"You didn't have to," she said. "That's what couples are supposed to do—"

"You're not my therapist, and we're not a couple." He closed the short space between them, internal fire neutralizing the low temperatures. The closer he inched, the more her personal gravitational pull on him intensified, to the point he knew if he wasn't careful, he might never back off. "You can cut the manipulative interest in my mental health. I'm here for one thing—to give that baby of yours a fighting chance." He pointed to her stomach. "If that means proving you're guilty, so be it. At least she'll grow up not knowing what kind of monster her mother really is."

"*Our* baby." Her gaze held his as she smoothed her hands over where her baby belly had started to appear. Raleigh stepped into him, pulling back her shoulders as though she were preparing for war. Hell, in a way, loving her had been war. They'd both brought out a competitiveness in each other and dedicated themselves to their work over their relationship. They might've been living together, but Raleigh had been dedicated to the foundation at the time, and he'd been on the road most days chasing bad guys. When it'd ended, neither of them had recognized the other anymore. It'd just taken seeing her arrest on the news that he'd realized how lonely they'd truly been together. How desperate for contact she'd made him. "You keep saying my baby, but she's ours, Beckett, and it took two of us to make her. That means you have as much responsibility here to protect her as I do, and that's what I'm trying to do. Protect her. With or without your help."

He froze, narrowing his gaze on her. "What's that supposed to mean?"

"I could've run, Beckett. Even with the cuffs on. I've got bags buried all over these woods that would get me out of Oregon." Her voice faltered. "You were asleep, and it would've been easy to run, but I didn't."

"Why not?" Criminals like her—like his father— did anything to keep from answering for what they'd done. Wasn't that why she'd escaped federal custody in the first place? Why he hadn't heard from Hank

Foster in over twenty years? Hell, he didn't even know if the old man was still alive. Didn't care. Raleigh was right. She could've run, but here she stood, going toe-to-toe with the man tasked to bring her in. "You had the chance. Why didn't you take it?"

Raleigh swept her tongue across her bottom lip as the last few drops of rain fell from her chin. "I don't want my daughter growing up without her parents. I don't want her to have the same kind of life I did. I didn't want her not knowing the people who are supposed to love her more than anything in this world or being passed around by anyone willing to take her on the off chance they might get a paycheck for their trouble. Do you have any idea what that's like, Beckett? To feel unwanted like that, to feel so worthless not even your own family wants to take you in?"

He'd known about her parents. Her mother had died a few days after giving birth to Raleigh and her twin brother, and no one in the state of Oregon seemed to know who had donated his fatherly genes to their creation. Their birth certificates had been left blank at the hospital, but Beckett hadn't known about the rest. The apparent hurt deepening the color of her eyes, so contrary to the fiery woman who'd pointed that shotgun at his chest back in her aunt's cabin, ripped at the edges of the hole she'd left behind in her wake. "Raleigh, I…"

He'd wanted her. More than anything—or anyone—else he could remember since he'd lost his mother. Hadn't she realized that? How desperate he'd been to keep her for himself? Constantly checking in with her while he'd been on the road, celebrating one-month, three-month and then six-month anniversaries. He'd been a regular romantic, and the drafted letter of resignation he'd stashed in his inner coat pocket revealed exactly how far he'd committed to go down with the ship. Just for a chance of hanging on to her a bit longer.

Beckett took a step back, his heel sinking in the mud, but no amount of distance from her could hide the truth. For as much as he'd blamed her for what'd happened between them, he'd never told her how much she'd meant to him, how afraid he'd been of losing her.

He'd lost everyone he'd cared about and been left to fend for himself from the time he'd been sixteen. He'd worked the ranch as best he could on his own for two years, graduated high school at the top of his class and started taking criminal justice courses before applying to the Marshals Service. No one had helped or been there for him after the shooting. Until Raleigh. She'd blazed into his life and set up residence beneath his skin. She'd shouldered the responsibility to take care of him when the nightmares came for him and never demanded answers. She'd been fearless, driven and everything he'd needed to leave the past behind. She'd been a constant he was willing to defend, and while she'd ripped his heart practically out of his chest when

she'd been arrested, the tiny life they'd created together deserved what he'd lost, what they'd both
lost: a family.

"I'm innocent, Beckett," she said. "But all I need
from you is to believe me."

Believe her. As if that would change anything.

"You've made your point. Neither of us wants
this baby born behind bars." Damn it. He was about
to do something stupid. Beckett scrubbed one hand
down his face as his entire career flashed before
his eyes. Guess that was to be expected when the
life you'd built died right in front of you, but some-
times you had to take the law into your own hands.
Only problem was, he'd gotten a good look at the
prosecution's case. The state had done a hell of a
job showing no one else at the foundation could've
taken that money. All they needed to close this investigation was the woman they'd pressed charges
against on the other side of the courtroom. Whatever evidence Raleigh believed was out there that
would prove her innocence had been buried deep
enough the FBI hadn't gotten their hands on it. That
was what they had to find. Fast. The US Marshals'
office—more specifically, his chief deputy, Remington "Remi" Barton—wouldn't sign off on in-
vestigating a case he wasn't assigned, especially
at the insistence of a suspect. Which meant he and
Raleigh had two days, maybe less, before his team
caught up. He wrapped one hand around her ban-

daged arm and removed the cuffs from her wrists with the other. "I'm going to regret this."

THE EVIDENCE BROUGHT UP against her was irrefutable.

Forged transfer documents, offshore accounts with her name listed as the owner, dates that coincided with her travel plans to meet with other nonprofit organizations across the country. It all pointed to her. Whoever had embezzled all that money knew exactly how to make the foundation— make her—hurt. This had been her life's work, the reason she'd put herself through business school and dedicated herself to changing the course of mortality rates for mothers across the globe. Only now it was all at risk. Everything she'd worked for would be destroyed if they couldn't clear her name, leaving nothing but death and loss in its wake if the foundation went under.

"Just a bit farther." Beckett took position up ahead, leading them west through the trees. "You got any more of your go bags around here? We're running low on water."

"No. I buried most of them north of the cabin. That was the route I was going to take if the Marshals ever caught up with me." She framed her near-invisible baby bump with her hands as they trudged through mud, fallen leaves and the occasional patch of twigs. It was silly. The baby wasn't any bigger than an artichoke right then, but Raleigh found comfort every time her palms pressed against the slightly hardened surface of her stomach. Her boots suctioned at the damper places in the ground, increasing the wear on her muscles when exhaustion had already stripped too much of her energy. Sweat built in her hairline with each step despite the fresh rush of cold in the air. Oregon had always been home, but out here in the middle of nowhere, with no cell coverage, board meetings or the incessant drone of the city, she'd found an invigorating peace she hadn't felt anywhere else. Well, almost anywhere else.

She lifted her attention from where she'd place her next step to the man who'd bandaged her wounds in the middle of a rainstorm while swearing he'd put her behind bars if she so much as thought about running again.

She'd almost forgotten the feel of his gaze on her, the raw intensity with which he handled himself. Then he'd touched her. One touch from him had ignited a sweeping heat deep inside her body she'd been craving since she'd been arrested. He'd cleaned the scratches on her arms with a care and gentleness nobody else had done for her. No matter what happened between them after the investigation was over, she wouldn't forget that. He'd always been cautious, defensive, suspicious even, but not with her. All that power, as though he intended to set anyone and anything on fire if it got in the way of justice, built under his cool exterior until it became too much to handle, but he never let it touch her. That was what made him a US marshal. Not the lifetime worth of education and training he'd gone through but the commitment to do the job in the first place, a deep-seated root of dedication he'd accrued long before he'd swept into her life.

"I need to take a break," she said.

Beckett settled those brilliant blue eyes on her, and her nerves hiked into awareness. The past twelve hours had shown her exactly how much had changed since she saw two blue lines on that drugstore pregnancy test, as well as the five that followed, and he slowed his pace. "We've got to keep moving."

"No, I get it. We're vulnerable out here in the open. There's just one problem with that." She bent at the knees and nearly doubled over as fiery bile worked up her throat. Forcing herself to take deep breaths, she closed her eyes as the leaves under her boots started to sway. And not from the wind. "I have to eat every couple of hours, or your daughter takes it out on me."

"Damn it." Calluses caught on the fabric of her shirt as he coursed one palm over her spine, and in an instant, the nausea's controlling grip eased. "I don't know how all this…you being pregnant works yet. I think we have some granola left. Let me find it."

"If it makes you feel any better, neither do I. This is all new for me, too. Every day is a new surprise." Raleigh reached for the boulder a few feet away and slid down onto it. The coolness bleeding through her jeans helped chase back the knot in her stomach, but it didn't compare to the savagery Beckett used emptying their pack in order to find her something to eat. In less than thirty seconds, he straightened, the thick muscles in his thighs flexing. She took the water and granola bar he offered, careful not to let her fingers come into contact with his as another wave of heat exploded through her insides. He'd made it perfectly clear things had ended between them when he'd refused to return her dozens of calls and messages after the arrest. She wasn't supposed to be noticing the way his veins fought to escape the skin along the backs of his hands as he pinched the top of his hat between his fingers and swept his hair back away from his face. Or was this sudden rush of awareness due to the pregnancy hormones? Didn't matter. Beckett Foster had made his choice, and it hadn't been her.

"Thanks." Draining the bottle, she tore into the granola, speaking around the food in her mouth. "You should drink up, too. It might be the middle of fall, but you're still sweating."

Dehydration would slow them down faster than her swollen, achy body would, but she wasn't about to admit that out loud. Definitely not to him.

"That was the last of it." He stared out into the trees, never making eye contact with her. Replacing his hat on his head, he shouldered their pack, as though the fact he'd given up the last of his water—their water—for her in a moment of exhausted weakness wasn't a big deal. "Unless we come across another of your buried packs, that's all we have until we reach the ranch."

"You didn't have to do that." She chewed the last of the granola bar, the oats and Craisins sticking along her throat. She wiped her mouth with the back of her hand and pushed upright. There were only a handful of properties out here on the other side of East Lake, most of which were owned by horse trainers or wheat farmers. Someone had already gotten to her cofounder, and a gunman had tried to kill her and Beckett less than twelve hours ago. They couldn't involve anyone else. Not without putting innocent lives in danger. "What ranch?"

"USMS manages half a dozen seized properties up and down these parts. The one we're closest to was seized from a drug dealer after we connected him to one of the southern cartels for pushing their product into Eugene." He waved his finger to the right. Beckett slowed his escape along the trail, his jacket shifting over powerful shoulders. Unpocketing his phone, he shook his head. "Don't expect anything fancy. We'll be lucky if there's still running water, but we'll at least have a roof over our heads and be in cell range so I can make contact with the rest of my team."

His team? Raleigh spread one hand under her abdominals as a shiver chased down her spine. She forced one foot in front of the other, fighting to keep up with his long strides, but the fear of going back…of being found before they had a chance to clear her name…tunneled deep. She stopped in her tracks. The confidence that'd waned since she'd realized she'd put him on the wrong end of her shotgun charged forward. She'd been living off the grid for months, and she hadn't made any mistakes. Not on her end. There was only one way that gunman would've been able to find her, and it wasn't a coincidence he'd shown up minutes after Beckett had located her. "You can't do that. You can't involve the Marshals' office."

An inner earthquake shook through her as he narrowed that steely gaze on her. He slowly turned to face her, and suddenly he seemed so much… bigger than he had when he'd offered her the last of his water. Suspicious. "I'm a United States marshal, and you're a fugitive. If my boss finds out I'm interfering with this case, I'll be charged with aiding and abetting a known criminal, and your baby won't just lose one parent. She'll lose us both. Is that what you want?"

"It was you," she said.

"What are you talking about?" Confusion cleared some of the tension from his expression, but he was still too close.

"I've been out here for four months. I've been off the grid, running my own investigation into who could've stolen that money while making sure none of what I uncovered connected back to me." She fought the urge to increase the space between them as a hint of rain and pine from his clothing filled her lungs. "Whoever shot at us... They shouldn't have been able to find me, Beckett."

"Then maybe you're not as good as you think you are." He swept his coat to either side of his hips, hands leveraged against the lean muscle she'd memorized under those clothes. "Maybe you made a mistake. Your name is on that sonogram you showed me. There's a chance someone in the doctor's office recognized your photo from the most wanted list and called it in."

It was a possibility, but the chances were slim. She'd been careful, met with the doctor after hours for a hefty price, altered her appearance for the nurses. Because it wasn't just her life at stake anymore. She had a daughter to think about now, and she would do whatever it took to make sure she got out of this unharmed. Raleigh raised her gaze to his, the knot in her stomach tight. "Or maybe someone knew about our past connection. Maybe whoever stole that money used you to make sure I'd never walk out of these woods alive."

Chapter Four

"Let me get this straight." The muscles down his spine seized up. He rolled his lips between his teeth and bit down, the rustic tang of blood sliding across his tongue. Spreading his hands palms-down in front of him, he studied her for a sign—anything—that could give him an idea of where the hell she was going with this. "Instead of considering you might've made a mistake and given up your location on your own, which, I'll add, wasn't too hard to predict, you're saying I'm responsible for what went down at your aunt's cabin."

"It's not hard to believe whoever framed me knew about our relationship and used that to their advantage, knew you'd follow those unwavering Boy Scout morals of yours to bring me in." She slid her hand along her lower abdominals, a nervous habit he bet she'd picked up somewhere between finding out she was pregnant and today. "I'd say whoever we're dealing with doesn't just know me. They've done their homework on you, too. They could've easily followed you with the intention of taking us both out to keep me from getting to the truth. They might even have a connection in the Marshals Service and made sure you were assigned my recovery."

The hairs on the back of his neck stood on end, but Beckett kept his expression smooth as her words registered. Finnick Reed, Jonah Watson and his chief deputy, Remi Barton. They'd all put their lives on the line for him on the job, just as he'd done for them over the past decade they'd been assigned to work together in the Oregon district office. Their team had apprehended a record number of fugitives, dismantled criminal enterprises and aided in more statewide manhunts than any other office on the West Coast. The four of them made up the backbone of the federal government, and he trusted every single one of them with his life. But the fact a shooter had tried to kill him and Raleigh less than fifteen minutes after Beckett had found her grated on his instincts. Damn it. He couldn't discount her theory. Hell, it was the only thing they had to go on right now, and that meant leaving his team out of the investigation. For now. "You obviously have someone in mind. Someone from your list of suspects at the foundation."

She nodded, stringy, damp hair skimming the bullet graze at the side of her neck, and it felt as though blood had pooled in his legs, cementing him in place. Another inch to the left and that bullet would've killed her. He would've lost her, lost their baby. This far out, with the closest hospital more than thirty miles away, he wouldn't have been able to save either of them, and his chest tightened at the imagery. "My assistant, Emily Cline. She's worked for me since the beginning and had access to the donations anytime I had to travel. She would've had the perfect opportunity to transfer those funds when I was guaranteed to be out of the office."

"I remember her from the background checks the feds ran. I assume she arranged all your travel, kept your schedule, had your bank account and Social Security numbers to arrange hotels and car rentals?" A cold bite of wind ripped through the trees, but it was the weary hint of exhaustion playing out across Raleigh's features that held his attention. It took everything inside him to keep himself from chasing back the dark circles under her eyes with the pad of his thumb.

She cast her attention to the gravel under her boots. "Out of all of the suspects I've compiled, Emily is the only one who had the means and opportunity to move that money, aside from Calvin, but I can't see the connection between her and the US Marshals Service. Maybe there isn't one. I don't know."

He hadn't gotten a good enough look at the shooter to rule Emily Cline out as a suspect, but having a name was a start. Looked like their only leads were an assistant who possibly knew too much and a missing CEO, but Beckett couldn't dig any deeper than that without alerting his team to what he and Raleigh were doing out here.

"You obviously trusted her," he said. "Did she give you any reason to think she might be in debt or in trouble? Taking care of a sick relative, or does she have access to a gun?"

"No. Nothing like that. We were...friends." Her voice softened, tugging at some invisible string Beckett had used to sew up the gaping holes she'd left behind when she'd been arrested, but that was as far as he'd let it go. This effect she still had on him, this gravitational pull, was nothing more than his body adjusting to being around her again. Temporary. That was it. As soon as they cleared her name of the embezzlement charges, they could each go their separate ways and work out a custody-and-visitation agreement along the way for their daughter. If they couldn't... Hell, he'd have to cross that bridge when he got to it. Raleigh tucked her hands in her front pockets. "At least, I thought we were friends. Guess it goes to show how little we actually know the people around us, or how blind we can make ourselves when we don't want to see the truth."

Was that supposed to be an underhanded accusation directed at him? Because she was right. They might've been sleeping together for six months, but they'd each kept the darkest part of themselves from the other. They didn't know each other at all. A bird called off to their right, then silence. Warning prickled a trail across his shoulders. He automatically drew her in to his side with one hand as he scanned the trees around them. He couldn't take the risk of another ambush from the shooter. Not with their daughter the perfect target. "Come on. We've been out in the open for too long."

She didn't respond, a first for her, as he led her along the unofficial path carving through the trees. The pines thinned after another twenty minutes of them walking in silence beside each other, giving way to one of the most exquisite sights Oregon had to offer. Jagged obsidian lava rock spread out along each side of the path they'd been following toward the smooth incline of Newberry volcano. Dark clouds cast shadows over the second lake in the area on the other side of the inactive caldera. From this vantage point, he calculated they'd walked approximately four miles around the southern end of East Lake and were nearing the Big Obsidian Flow Trailhead. Miles of green pines smothered the valley floor below, and a lightness he hadn't felt in a long time spread through him.

"My brother and I used to hike out here every weekend when we got the chance. Just the two of us." A wistful smile transformed her features, and for a split second, his heart jerked in his chest at the sight. Her shoulders rose and fell with her heavy breathing, that warm gaze taking it all in. "We'd pack a lunch, bring our swimsuits and make sure the rangers weren't around when we climbed the volcano. I forgot how beautiful this place can be."

"You haven't been back out here?" He wasn't sure why he'd asked, or why he cared much about the answer. The lines between them had been drawn, but every second she'd been near, he could feel that old part of himself—the part that wanted to believe her—rise to the surface.

"Not since he died. I thought about it. I wanted to see if it'd changed any, but…it's not the same without him." Smoothing her hands over her shirt, she shook her head, long tendrils of her hair sticking to the fabric. Raleigh turned toward him, resurrecting the atmospheric hint of rain and her vanilla scent in one move. "Earlier, you said you unsealed my juvenile records, but did you read them?"

"I read enough of the police report to know what happened that day. I was able to piece together the rest." In reality, there hadn't been a whole lot to read. He'd had to track down the autopsy report himself. "Your aunt had taken custody of you both at the insistence of your and your brother's social worker because you kept getting passed from home to home. Reports said you had trouble adjusting. You instigated a handful of fights and were caught stealing from one of your foster parents. Am I right so far?"

The muscles along the column of her throat worked to swallow. "Keep going."

"You, your brother and your aunt were down at

the shoreline of the lake. Police found a couple easy chairs, a picnic and an umbrella. The scene looked like it was supposed to be a fun day, but there was a fight. Something your aunt did made you snap." He set his hands on his hips, the bottom of the pack she'd dug up brushing against the space between his index finger and thumb. "You caved her skull in with a rock you found in the water."

She flinched, obviously not ready to hear just how much he'd uncovered about her past, but she couldn't hide from it anymore. Couldn't hide the truth from him. She'd kept her secrets to herself when they'd been together, but Beckett knew her better than anyone else in her life, was the only one who knew exactly what she was capable of. Innocent people didn't run, didn't go into hiding. They didn't hurt the people who cared about them. Directing her attention back out across the valley as the wind rustled in the trees on either side of them, she ran one hand through her hair. "That's all the files say? The police report, the court documents?"

"It's enough, isn't it?" he asked. "Proves you have a history of violence and theft, which, I might add, is what you're up against now, and that you're willing to do whatever it takes to get what you want, even when it hurts the people who care about you."

"You're right. My brother and I were eating lunch together like we always did on the weekends. I wasn't feeling too good that day. I think I was coming down with the flu or something, so he said we should set up down on the beach instead of taking our normal hike, and I agreed. I didn't care where we went. I just wanted to spend time with him. For as long as I remember, we were all we had. Then…" She blinked against the sunlight reflecting off the water of Paulina Lake about a mile northeast of their location. "Then my aunt came charging down to the lake, accusing my brother of getting into her gun safe. I'd never seen her so angry before, and no matter what I said, she didn't believe me."

"Because it was you." Memory of the cabin, of the open armored safe tucked into the room off the main living space, flashed across his mind. Dread curled in his gut. Hell. "You were the one who'd gotten into the safe, weren't you?"

"I'd learned to break into it a few weeks before by listening for the click of the combination cams, and I was so damn proud of myself, I wanted to see if I could do it again." She stared out over the expanse of trees and water. "My brother was everything to me, the only person I'd always been able to count on growing up in all those homes, the only one I had left, and suddenly she was choking the life right out of him in front of my eyes." Nodding, she rolled her lips between her teeth and bit down, as though to keep herself under control, but he could see the pain in her eyes, the crack of emotions bleeding through her expression. Raleigh wiped at her face with one hand. "I tried to pull her off, but she hit me in the face, and I fell back into the water. I wasn't strong enough to pry her loose, so I grabbed a rock I'd landed on, and I swung it as hard as I could." Green eyes focused on him. "But it was too late. She'd already killed him."

He cleared his throat, completely void of a response other than an apology for what she'd been through at such a young age. Guess they both had that in common. Her losing her brother, him losing his mom.

"All those accusations you have of me starting fights and stealing? I was making sure my brother and I stayed together every time we got transferred to a new home. We only had each other, but none of it mattered in the end. I lost him anyway, and now I have no one." Loose gravel slipped down the rocky incline as she stepped into him. "Everything I've done hasn't been to hurt the people I care about, Beckett. It's been to protect them, and I'd do it all over again."

He stared after her as she made her way down the steep hill dropping them onto the main trail carved through the trees, his voice low. "You had me."

THE HUMIDITY OF another imminent downpour stuck to the exposed skin under her collar as they followed the Big Obsidian Flow Trailhead around the southern end of Paulina Lake. This time of year didn't bring a lot of tourists to the area, and she'd never been more grateful for that than now. The idea of pasting another smile on her face, of pretending everything was okay, even for a stranger, intensified the headache at the base of her skull. Sweat built along her hairline and slid down her spine, but she only pushed herself harder.

Those records had been sealed. She'd moved on with the intention of never letting those two adrenaline-charged minutes of her life define her. She'd given everything she'd had left after the incident with her aunt from that time forward to save lives. Not take them, but now Beckett knew the truth. The one person she'd tried to shield from her past knew she was everything he'd accused her of being: a killer. The fist around her heart squeezed tighter. There was nothing she could say, nothing she could do, to redeem herself in his eyes.

"We're here." His words punctured through the sweaty haze that'd taken over for the past hour, and Raleigh pulled up short too fast. Her boots slid along a loose patch of gravel on the incline leading down into a valley nestled between the mountains, and she fell back, arms thrown out for balance. Strong hands caught her under her rib cage. "I've got you."

A warmth that hadn't been there before blossomed inside as she tried to get her bearings. "Thanks."

Setting her upright, Beckett let his hand linger at her waist as she pressed into his chest for balance. Her heart thumped wildly at the base of her throat as his gaze journeyed a trail down along her neck. His outdoors scent dived deep into her lungs, making her lips tingle to close that short distance between them. She could still remember what he tasted like, how safe she'd felt in his arms.

Thunder clapped overhead. A drizzle of rain pelted her face from above, bringing her back into reality. He'd cleaned and bandaged the small scrapes along her forearms from the tree bark and given her the last of their water when she'd gotten light-headed, but none of that healed the invisible wound left behind by his indifference. He was here to bring her back into federal custody, and he'd offered to help because she happened to be carrying his child. Nothing more. Any promises that fell from that mouth, so close to hers, didn't mean anything. She couldn't let them mean anything.

Distancing herself from his comforting weight pressed against her, Raleigh surveyed the seemingly abandoned property fenced out at least a quarter mile back. Two large pines towered over the bright red farmhouse trimmed in white. A few other structures, smaller than the main house, interrupted the smooth expanse of green grass across the flat land. There was a detached garage; maybe even a second, although smaller, house; a large barn and a chicken coop. She followed the outline of white vinyl fencing that disappeared into the tree line off to the right. No visible vehicles. No animals. Nothing within a few miles. She was used to isolation, good at keeping to herself, but if the shooter who'd

followed Beckett really did have some kind of connection inside the Marshals Service, there was a
chance that isolation could be used against them.
"You're sure this place can't be traced back to you?"

"I was one of the marshals who seized the property from the previous owner. That's how I know
about this place, but USMS owns the deed. Unless
whoever tried to kill us can get into one of the most
secure federal databases in the country, there's no
way they'd know this place exists." He adjusted his
hat, then headed down the smooth slope leading
to the main house, lean muscle flexing along the
length of his hamstrings. "We'll be safe here while
we come up with a plan to get to your assistant. It
won't be easy. The FBI will be watching her, waiting to see if you make contact."

She followed close on his heels, hyperaware of
every move he made, every scan of the property,
every change in his expression. Beckett Foster had
one of the highest recovery-and-protection rates his
branch of law enforcement had ever seen. If there
was a threat, he'd be the first to see it coming. She
had to believe that. Had to believe that even though
her past had wedged this distance between them,
he'd do whatever it took to protect their daughter.

The ground leveled out under her as they approached the farmhouse's front door, and her fingers automatically curled into her palms. Exposed
wood pillars added to the country feel lining the
wood wraparound porch, large windows peering

out over the rest of the property. Glancing in, she searched the first level of the two-story structure but couldn't see anything more than a few pieces of furniture, crisply painted white walls and the floor-to-ceiling windows at the back of the home. No movement inside. Nothing to suggest he was walking her into a federal ambush made up of marshals and FBI agents, but she wouldn't discount the possibility.

Beckett keyed in a code on the electronic keypad where a dead bolt usually fit, and the sound of a lock disengaging reached her ears. He swung the door inward, motioning her inside past him and the raw wood door at his back. The weight of his attention pressurized the air in her lungs as she stepped over the threshold. "You can get settled in the larger of the two bedrooms on the main floor while I check the perimeter. Shouldn't take more than a few minutes."

"Okay." She nodded, not knowing what else to say as she took in the large expanse of the main living space. Dark wood flooring stretched the length of the house all the way back to the windows she'd spotted before, with bright white couches and a modern wood-and-metal coffee table set between them. Blue chairs caught her eye from the dining room table beside two more support columns welcoming guests into the modern kitchen. Hard to believe a drug smuggler had run his business for the cartel through a home this beautiful. It looked too…welcoming. Homey.

Beckett closed the door behind him, leaving her alone for the first time since he'd broken into her aunt's cabin, and an instant hollowness fisted in her gut. Which didn't make any sense. He'd ripped through her life as quickly as a hurricane, leaving her decimated, ruined and empty. The pain— the longing—she'd felt after he'd walked away shouldn't have dug its claws in this deep. She was supposed to be an ocean, able to survive anything, supposed to withstand the strength of the storm, but then she'd heard him yelling in his sleep. And everything inside her had broken. The walls she'd built, the anger she'd held on to… They'd evaporated as fast as clouds shifted in the sky. In that moment, with her hand over his heart soothing small circles into his chest, the past had sped up to meet the present.

Raleigh folded her arms across her midsection.

Modern black-and-white tile adorned the fireplace off to her left. Her fingers and toes tingled with the need for warmth, but that was nothing compared to the heat still burning through her from when Beckett had placed his hands on her hips after she'd slipped. It was one thing to ask for his help, but to hole up under the same roof again while a shooter hunted them down trailed goose bumps across her chest. She trod deeper into the house, passing the kitchen and a small home office until she came to the first bedroom in the long stretch of hallway. She ached at the sight of the bed, but she couldn't let down her guard yet. They were out of food, out of water, and their only lead had already been questioned and investigated by the FBI before Raleigh had been arrested. If her assistant was responsible for framing Raleigh for taking that money, the feds would've uncovered the evidence.

She ran her hands through her snarled hair, the ends frizzing with the added humidity outside. Light gray wallpaper and navy bedcovers urged her to close her eyes. She slipped onto the edge of a pale padded bench at the end of the bed, skimming her palms down her jeans. The same flooring in the main part of the house ran lengthwise through this room, same color of white upholstery giving a serene, peaceful feeling to the entire house.

Peace. When was the last time she'd felt something even remotely close to peace?

She wanted to sink into it. Wanted to believe nothing outside this room existed, that she hadn't been falsely charged with fraud and embezzlement, that there wasn't a killer targeting her. Raleigh studied the streaks of water trailing down the large windows. What would it be like to live here? Raise her daughter here? What would it be like to wake up next to Beckett in this very bed? Raleigh moved to smooth the wrinkles from the deep-colored comforter but hesitated at the sight of the dirt still caking her hands and fingernails. No. This wasn't her bed. This wasn't her house. This wouldn't ever be her life. Not as long as she was a fugitive.

Not as long as Beckett only saw her as a criminal.

"The perimeter's secure." Footsteps echoed down the hallway before mesmerizing blue eyes settled on her, and her heart gave a small jerk in her chest. The traitor. "And we now have running water and power after a small, but very serious, electric shock I wasn't prepared for."

"Beckett, I…" She pushed up off the bed. The life they'd had together, their relationship, had been equally ripped right out from under them, and there was nothing they could do to get it back. Beckett would never let himself see her as anything more than the enemy he'd dedicated his career—his life—to hunting, and she was so tired of watching the people who'd claimed they cared walk away. She'd given everything to hang on to him after her arrest until it'd felt as though her heart had dried up. Too much had changed between them. She'd changed, but neither of them would be able to walk away from this unharmed. For the first time in a long time, she wasn't willing to sacrifice what was left of herself to hold on to that hope she could fix this. Gravity increased its grip on her at the realization, the desertlike cracks left over from heartbreak filling. "I'm sorry. For all of this. You had every right to distance yourself from me after my arrest. You were protecting yourself, and I understand that now. It was wrong of me to put you in that position in the first place, but I need you to believe I wasn't reaching out to you to use your job with the Marshals to my advantage. I just needed...you. You were all I had left."

He lowered his attention to the floor. No response.

"I can't keep running. I'm going to be a mom in a few months, and the only way I can do that job justice is to make this baby girl a priority and to give her a life she deserves. Give her some stability." She smoothed her palms over her still-damp shirt, but reassurance didn't surface this time. "Even if that means her growing up without me."

Beckett shot his head up, locked his gaze on her. "What is that supposed to mean?"

"Whoever framed me for taking that money is powerful, Beckett. They'd covered all their bases and made sure the evidence pointed to me. This doesn't feel like some desperate move to steal millions of dollars of donation money. It's personal. It's outright destruction. They've planned every move from the beginning, and they're obviously willing to kill me in order to make sure everything goes according to that plan. I'm not going to risk this baby's or your life for the smallest chance of proving I'm innocent." The muscles in her jaw ached with the pressure from her back teeth. "I want you to bring me in. You'll have full custody after she's born. Just...promise me to make sure she's loved, and that she knows I did everything I could for her."

"You told me you could prove you're innocent,

and now you want me to bring you in." Strong fingers encircled her arm, tugging her into a wall of muscle. She pressed her palms against his chest, his heart thudding hard beneath her hands. "What's changed?"

"Beckett, this is the only way to make sure you and the baby are safe." Raleigh sucked in a deep breath, and her throat dried. "I've lost too many people in my life. I can't handle the thought of losing her. And…I won't lose you."

"No one is taking you from me. Not again." He crushed his mouth to hers.

Chapter Five

She was willing to turn herself in to protect their baby. To protect him.

The guilty ran, but they never surrendered.

Beckett had been fully committed to giving in to the anger and distance that'd been swirling inside him for the past four months, but then she'd up and asked him to bring her in to the feds. To raise their baby on his own. He wasn't sure what'd happened next other than knowing, deep down, he wasn't ready to let her go that easily, and he had pulled her right into him and kissed her.

He opened his mouth wider, took everything she had to give and more. Slipping both arms around Raleigh, he pulled her against him as tight as humanly possible. An explosion of need seared through him as he consumed her. Enough to decimate everything he'd been holding on to since her arrest. The anger, the betrayal, the fear of the past, of realizing the person he'd trusted the most had become nothing more than a common criminal. Reckless, untamed desire for the woman in his arms took control to the point he barely had enough sense to pull away to take a breath.

Damn it. She was everything he remembered, everything he'd wanted, and he wasn't sure it was possible to ever get enough of her. These past few months—the isolation, the loneliness—disappeared in an instant as she penetrated the seam of his mouth with her tongue, and the entire world threatened to drop right out from under him.

She gasped as he trailed his mouth along the tendon at her throat, fingers fisting in his shirt for balance. "Beckett."

His name on her lips only intensified the craze singing through his veins. Lean muscle flexed under his fingers as he maneuvered them back toward the single bed. A feral growl escaped his throat as she threaded her fingers through his hair and re-directed his mouth to hers. Capturing his bottom lip between her teeth, she bit down, and electricity lightninged down his spine. No matter how many times he'd tried to move on, to forget her, she was just so damn perfect. Compelling, passionate and wild. Every cell in his body wanted every cell in hers, and he didn't have the strength to pull away.

Her knees hit the edge of the mattress, and the muscles down her spine tensed under his touch. "Beckett, we need to stop. This isn't…this isn't what I want."

He gripped her hips, drawing back. His lungs

battled to keep up with his racing heart rate, his entire body lit up from a single brush of her mouth against his. Raw. Unbalanced. Warmth swirled in those green eyes, and his gut clenched with unsatisfied desire. Dimly, he understood this was a bad idea. He was a marshal tasked with bringing her in to answer for not appearing before the judge, and while they were having a baby together, that didn't make his job any less of a reality. She was right. She couldn't keep running, couldn't hide forever. That wasn't the kind of life either of them wanted for this baby. "You're right."

He sucked in a breath between his teeth as she swept her tongue along the edges of her mouth. Why couldn't they go back to before she'd been arrested? To the moment when neither of them had been anything more than two people intent on living out the rest of their lives together. No secrets. No lies. No careers driving them apart. What they'd had together then hadn't been flawless, but it couldn't compare to any other personal encounter he'd experienced. She'd been a bright light in a sea of past darkness. For a while, she'd been his.

"I shouldn't have kissed you. I'm sorry. I…" Missed this connection. Missed her. Running one hand through his hair, Beckett put space between them, their exhalations mingling for a few breaths. No matter how this investigation ended, it'd never be the same as it once was. There was too much history between them, too much doubt.

He'd meant what he had said before. He'd fight like hell to ensure nobody—not even the US Marshals Service—could take her and this baby from him, but his offer of protection couldn't equate to anything more than that. Partnerships thrived on trust, and until they were able to prove she had nothing to do with those stolen donation funds, he couldn't trust her. "It won't happen again."

"I think that's for the best." Nodding, Raleigh swiped the back of her hand against her kiss-stung lips, the slight hint of brown sugar from the granola settling on his tongue. She hiked her thumb toward one of the closed doors attached to the bedroom. "I'm going to shower before we figure out our next move. It's been a rough couple of days, and it's going to take a while to get all this dirt off."

Their next move. Right. Because there was still a gunman out there ready to rip her and their baby out of his life, and they only had one lead when it came to clearing her name of the embezzlement charges.

"Good idea. In the meantime, I'll see if I can find us something to eat." And maybe run off the heat still simmering under his skin to cool down in the rain. What the hell had he been thinking, kissing her like that? He'd set the lines between them, and it'd taken less than twenty-four hours for him to break his own rules. Guess that'd always been the problem when it came to Raleigh. He hadn't been thinking. Not when he'd run to help her during the mugging all those months ago. Not when they'd fallen into bed together that same night, and not when he'd almost handed in his resignation from the Marshals after her arrest. Beckett headed toward the hallway and started to close the bedroom door behind him. Distance. He needed to clear his head, and he sure as hell wasn't going to get the chance sticking around here.

"Beckett, wait." Her voice slipped through the crack in the door, and the hairs on the back of his neck stood on end.

He slowed. Long, dirt-stained fingers wrapped around the edge of the door to pry it wider. Perfectly shaped brows smudged with dirt, a shallow laceration across one sharp cheekbone, light pink lips with a bit of beard burn on one corner. None of it took away from the flawless beauty and strength underneath as she leveled those mesmerizing green eyes on him. She toyed with the bandages he'd secured along her forearms.

"You saved my life, even though I'm sure it was the last thing on your mind," she said. "If you hadn't been there when that gunman tried to shoot me, I'm not sure I'd be standing here, and I wanted to thank you. For protecting us."

Hell, no matter how many times he'd convinced himself he had her pegged, she'd deliver a devastating uppercut and sucker punch him with the unexpected. Raleigh wasn't innocent, not in the least, but she sure wasn't acting like a criminal either, and he had no idea what to do with that information. "Part of the job."

"Is that all this is to you? What this baby and me are? A job?" A wave of vulnerability cracked through her carefully controlled expression as though he'd somehow gotten beneath her skin, but Beckett had been played before. Every change in body language, every look, every sweep of her hands over her stomach was meant to manipulate and confuse him. This intelligent, ambitious, beautiful woman only wanted one thing: to survive. He knew better than to believe any of what she'd told him had been used for anything other than getting her way. She only let him see what she wanted him to see, same game as his old man played until the day Hank got up and left Beckett and his mother behind, and he wasn't going to let himself fall prey again.

"I'll be back to check on you in twenty," he said. "There're alarm sensors on all the windows, so I'd stay away from them if I were you. Can't be too careful."

The fine lines between her brows smoothed. "Thanks for the advice, Marshal."

She pushed the door closed, the lock engaging loud in his ears. The sound of water hitting tile registered through the thin wood a few seconds later. He gripped his hand around the doorknob to keep himself from barging back in that room and telling her the truth. He had to focus. They had one chance to get to Emily Cline, Raleigh's assistant, without alerting the feds or the Marshals Service he'd found his fugitive, and he wasn't going to waste it.

A loud trill cut through the tension-charged haze in his head, and Beckett reached for the phone in his back pocket. Saved by the bell. He swiped the green button to answer the call as his boss's name registered and brought the phone to his ear. "Remington, what can I do for you?"

"Deputy Foster." Disappointment slid into the chief deputy's voice and pooled dread at the base of his spine. So much for holding off his team. "I'm surprised you answered the phone. Seems like you've hit a snag in your recovery assignment of Raleigh Wilde."

Beckett leaned one shoulder into the wall beside him, folding one arm across his chest. The butt of his weapon scraped along his forearm. "Why on earth would you think that?"

"I'm going to let you figure that one out on your own." Finnick Reed and Jonah Watson, damn fine marshals he'd worked countless cases with, and they'd just been sent in to take over his. Damn it. "I've got an unregistered vehicle that once belonged to Ms. Wilde's deceased aunt parked next to your SUV at a cabin out at East Lake, bullet casings near the tree line, two sets of footprints heading into the woods, and another leading to a set of tire tracks we haven't been able to identify."

His back teeth ached from the pressure in his jaw, and Beckett straightened. Of all the successful fugitive recoveries he'd worked over the past decade, she'd brought in two other marshals? "You sent them to check up on me."

"Wouldn't you in my position?" Remi asked. "I gave you this assignment because you told me you could handle it, but from the crime-scene photos I'm looking at, that doesn't seem to be the case at all. Tell me I'm wrong, Beckett. Tell me you're not on the run with a known fugitive in some last-ditch effort to fix what went wrong between the two of you, and I'll reassign Watson and Reed another case."

Beckett turned toward Raleigh's door, her earlier question still echoing through his head. Was this just a case to him? Or more? Remington Barton hadn't gotten to her position as chief deputy of the USMS Oregon district office by avoiding the tough conversations or backing down from the challenges she'd faced as a female in their chosen profession. She was confident, persuasive and one of the best marshals he'd ever had the pleasure of working beside. She wasn't going to let this go. He tightened his grip around the phone. The second he revealed Raleigh was pregnant with his kid, Remi would order him out of the field and pull in another marshal for the recovery.

No. This wasn't just another case to him. Never had been. Not when it came to the woman on the other side of that door. He'd given Raleigh his word to see this through, to protect her and the baby, and that was exactly what he was going to do. But, more than that, that familiar scent of hers woven into his clothes, the feel of her soothing circles on his chest after he'd woken up from another fresh nightmare... She helped settle the agitation and restlessness permanently etched into his bones, and for the first time in longer than he wanted to admit, he felt like he could finally breathe. Who else had been able to do that for him but her?

"Beckett?" Remi asked. "Tell me I'm wrong."

Beckett slid his shoulder up the wall and straightened. "You're wrong."

He ended the call.

SEARING HEAT TRAILED along her skin and cleared the dirt and leaves from her scalp, but no amount of hot water could make her forget that kiss. She...hadn't expected that. And she hadn't stopped it either. She and Beckett had been together for six months before her arrest, but that kiss had taken her by surprise. Electrically charged, heated, almost starved. She could still feel the bruising indentations of his fingers in her lower back as he'd fought to bring her closer. Almost like he'd been missing a puzzle piece and wanted her to fill the empty space. The difference between the man she'd been with before her arrest and the one who'd kissed her as though he hadn't been able to breathe unless connected to her mouth still rocked through her. Raleigh brushed the pads of her fingers across her lips, flinching at the immediate sting at one side. *No one is taking you from me.*

Taking her from him? Or taking the baby?

She stepped from the shower, air from the vent above fighting to cool the frantic rush of desire still heating her from head to toe—in vain. Drying off with one of the towels hanging nearby, she wrapped herself in a robe dangling on the back of the bathroom door. The same tile that'd lined the fireplace in the main living room added to the modern farmhouse feel of the bathroom. Her reflection skewed in gold light fixtures and plumbing as she ran her fingers through her freshly washed hair.

Didn't matter what he'd meant before, or why he'd kissed her. No matter how much she wanted his presence and intentions to be for her, he'd made it clear that wasn't the case. He was here to do a job, and she couldn't let their past—however short it'd been—cloud her judgment now. She'd worked too hard to distance herself from falling back into old patterns, especially when it came to relying on others. She'd fight to clear her name of the fraud and embezzlement charges, with or without his help, move on with her life, and give this baby the life and love she deserved. She'd gotten by this far on her own. She'd learned to be strong, resilient, driven. Having Beckett here didn't change that.

Raleigh stepped into the large walk-in closet attached to the bathroom, running her fingers through the clothes that'd been left behind by who she assumed were the previous owners of the house before the marshals had seized the property. Dark suit jackets, white shirts and an array of colorful ties hung on one side, the other filled with silk scarves, brand labels, heels and lingerie. Checking back over her shoulder, she skimmed her fingers across the soft fabrics and lace. Her arrest had forced her to leave her possessions behind, including all of her clothing, just as this couple had been forced. She'd worn the dirt-caked jeans, flannel shirt and cotton underwear from her aunt's cabin in desperation. She'd discarded them on the unique tile a few feet away, but she couldn't stand the thought of putting them back on. Not after reliving the gut-wrenching memory of her brother's last moments.

She wasn't desperate anymore. She didn't have to rely on the pain, anger and resources from the past to carry her through the present. Because she wasn't alone this time. Her heart jerked in her chest as footsteps echoed down the hallway toward the bedroom door.

Three quick knocks accompanied that deep, all-too-familiar voice. "Raleigh, you okay?"

She pulled back her shoulders to counteract the instant warmth pooling at the base of her spine. She wasn't physically alone anymore, but emotionally? She couldn't depend on anyone but herself. "I'll be out in a minute."

"Okay," Beckett said. "I found us something to eat when you're ready."

His boots echoed off the dark hardwood flooring installed throughout the house at his retreat, but the flood of heat refused to drain from her system. He'd always had that effect on her. One word, one touch, and an internal explosion destroyed her all over again without warning. But she'd meant what she'd said. She appreciated his help, but she couldn't afford the distraction getting involved with him offered. Not with their baby's life at stake.

Checking the label of the chunky dark green cable sweater in front of her, she tugged it from its position on top of a row of shelving. The sweater cost more than three months' salary at the foundation, but it fit, and she wasn't about to turn down clean clothes. A fresh start. She pulled a pair of black leggings, a white T-shirt and a set of nude lace lingerie from the drawers stacked against one wall and dressed quickly. The bra-and-panty set wasn't practical for surviving a gunman in the middle of the Oregon wilderness, but it'd been the least sexy item compared to the rest of the options in those drawers. Besides, it wasn't like anyone was going to see it but her. Least of all Beckett Foster.

Facing the mirror, she ran her fingers through her hair once again, but there seemed to be a lightness— a glow—to her skin now. Whether it was from the rush of heat from Beckett's kiss, or something… deeper, she didn't know. Didn't care. Scooping her dirty clothes from the floor, she deposited them into the garbage can under the vanity and shut the cabinet door. Mentally and physically. She had to move on, had to give this baby a real shot of happiness.

She had to leave the past behind.

Raleigh followed the maze of hallways back into the custom chef's kitchen. White cabinets adorned with gold fixtures surrounded a large steel fridge. The island became the focus of the entire space with navy blue shiplap and cascading white marble down each side as Beckett set two plates on the surface. For an instant, she was back in the bedroom, wondering what it'd be like to wake up to this sight every morning, live here, raise a family here.

Beckett half turned toward her. "You want cheese and crackers with deli turkey or a grilled cheese sandwich? I wasn't sure what you or the baby would be in the mood for, so I made both."

"Is it embarrassing to admit I want to eat all of it?" A laugh bubbled past her lips, something foreign since… She couldn't remember how long.

"Oh. Guess you're technically eating for two, right?" He focused his attention on the fridge, his hands flat on the marbled island. "Okay. I can eat the pickles Reed left in the fridge. He's the only one who likes the damn things."

"I'm joking." She threw one hand out, palm first, as another laugh escaped her chest. "Partly. I could eat it all, but I'll take the sandwich. Deli meat is frowned upon when pregnant."

A smile tugged at the corners of her mouth. When was the last time someone had made her something to eat? While she wasn't sure what Beckett had put together would last long between the two of them, he'd obviously put thought into it, having cut the sandwich down the middle to make it easier to eat. Her stomach clenched at the sight of gooey yellow cheese running over the edges of toasted, buttery bread, but she couldn't drown the thought that none of this was for her. Not really.

He'd cleaned her wounds, given up the last of his water, offered his protection. All of it because of the baby. Not out of any kind of loyalty or feelings for her. So then why had he kissed her? "You happened to have cheese, bread and cold cuts here?"

"Two marshals from my office were here a couple days ago installing new dead bolts and sensors." He handed her the plate with the grilled cheese sandwich and turned back toward the fridge. "When we seize a property, we like to make sure the previous owners can't get back in."

"I don't suppose they'll mind I borrowed some of their clothes, then." She took a seat on one of the distressed-metal bar stools as silence settled between them.

Beckett turned his head partially toward her.

"I'm sorry about your brother. I didn't realize how many details were missing from the police reports, and I made assumptions about you I shouldn't have." Setting two water bottles onto the countertop, he skidded one toward her. He leveraged both hands wide against the cold surface of the island, gaze down, and her skin prickled. "My father stole millions of dollars from hardworking Americans when I was a kid by getting them to invest in his Ponzi scheme." He twisted the cap off the bottled water and swallowed several mouthfuls. Strong muscles along his throat flexed and released. He set the bottle down carefully, then dented the plastic in a strong grip, knuckles fighting for release through the back of his hand. "They didn't have any clue he'd been stealing from them for years until the feds caught wind. They trusted him with their hard-earned money, depended on him to ensure they had a future, then lost everything in the blink of an eye. That's why I became a marshal. I've been hunting him ever since, but I lost his trail soon after he dropped off the radar."

The muscles down her spine hardened vertebra by vertebra. Her mouth dried as the nail he'd driven into her heart when he'd disappeared after her arrest settled deeper. She sat a bit straighter, not sure how to respond, what to say. "You've never talked to me about your family. Before…"

"I don't have a family." His voice graveled. "Hank Foster made sure of that when one of the people he swindled came looking for him and shot and killed my mother instead."

What? A forgotten sensation spread through her with a deep inhalation. Something she hadn't felt since that first time she'd realized he was never going to return her messages or her calls after she'd been arrested. That he was never going to live up to his promise to stay by her side, no matter what happened. Breathlessness overwhelmed her control. His mother had been murdered? Why hadn't he told her? She could've done something—anything—to help him through that pain, to support him, to comfort him, but he'd kept it all to himself. Why? With her next breath, the answer slipped to the tip of her tongue. He hadn't revealed that part of his past for the same reason she hadn't told him about her brother up front: to bury the darkness deep, to hide from it. But there was no hiding for either of them. Not anymore. "Beckett, I'm so sorry. How old—"

"Sixteen." He let go of the bottle, the plastic making a cracking sound with the sudden release of pressure. "After I found out about your arrest, I was right back there. I was that sixteen-year-old kid witnessing the damage a single act could inflict on so many lives firsthand, and done by someone I trusted, no less. Someone I thought cared about me."

Air stalled in her throat. He'd really believed she'd stolen that money. Not because of the prosecution's case pristinely wrapped in shiny paper but because he'd already learned the people who were supposed to care about him could turn on him at the drop of a hat. The same lesson she'd learned when her aunt had taken the single most important person in her life away. Twenty-four hours ago, they'd stood on the opposite sides of the law, but it seemed they weren't that different after all. Her fingers tingled as Raleigh reached across the cold marble and wrapped her hand in his. Blue eyes blazed at the contact, but she wouldn't pull away. Not this time. "I cared about you—"

A bullet exploded through the window above the kitchen sink.

And found its mark.

Chapter Six

"Beckett!"

Raleigh's voice pierced through the sudden rush of pain, and he held on to that invisible anchor as tight as he could while reaching for his service weapon. A flash of movement registered through the darkness closing in around the edges of his vision. Raleigh. He had to get her out of here, had to get her somewhere safe.

Long fingers pried him from off the cold marble island, the surface no longer white. She pulled him into her and forced him to sit against the oven's stainless-steel surface. Hell. The shooter who'd ambushed them at the cabin had caught up with them. Beckett locked his back teeth as another wave of agony rolled through his shoulder. The bullet hadn't gone straight through. If it had, he wouldn't have been the only one bleeding out. "You have to go. Get out of here. I'll hold them off as long as I can."

"That better be the blood loss talking. I'm not leaving you here to fight a gunman alone." She pressed her hands on either side of his shoulder, trying to apply pressure to the wound, but it wouldn't do him any good right now. They had to keep moving. He had to keep her and the baby safe. Raleigh glanced up over the countertop, toward the window the bullet had shattered on the way into his shoulder. "You've been shot. Tell me what to do."

"Find something in this kitchen I can use to stop the bleeding." He set his head back against the cool steel behind him, and a bit of the pain ebbed. He nodded toward four drawers stacked one over the other on one side of the island. "That should help long enough for us to get out of here. Try those drawers."

Keeping low to the ground, she crawled on her hands and knees and opened one drawer after the other. Her hands left bloody prints on the pale hardwood, and his insides jerked. She was wasting time she didn't have. The shooter had taken the shot that would leave Raleigh the most unprotected, and it was only a matter of time before their attacker tried to force their way inside to get to her.

"I don't want to think about why they have this in the kitchen, but it's the best we've got." She faced him, sliding back toward him on both knees, and held out a length of clear plastic tubing. With quick, sure movements, she wrapped the tubing around the space between his shoulder and neck and below his armpit, then lifted her gaze to his. Waiting. At his nod, she tightened the makeshift tourniquet as hard as she could, and white streaks shot across his vision.

A scream escaped up his throat. Latching on to her hand, he leveraged his heels into the floor and pressed his back against the oven as hard as he could to compensate for the pain. He couldn't afford to pass out. Not as long as there was an active shooter out there targeting the woman at his side. She adjusted her grip in his hand, the pain draining the longer she held on to him, but he didn't have time to wonder how that was possible. Neither of them did. He knocked his head back into the oven. "Damn it all to hell. The next time that bastard shoots at me, he better put me down."

"You said the other marshals on your team installed new locks and alarm sensors on all the doors and windows." Placing her hands alongside his rib cage, she helped pull him to his feet, and his heart rate hiked into overdrive. Hints of the shampoo she'd used in the shower dived into his lungs, something sweet. Like lavender and honey. "Tell me that will be enough to keep the shooter out."

Beckett clamped a hand to his shoulder, the gun heavy in his grip. "As long as the power is on—"

An audible electrical surge reached his ears.

Turning toward the now blank LED light over the burners on the stovetop, he pulled his phone from his jeans with his injured hand and tapped the screen. No service. Maneuvering Raleigh behind him, Beckett stepped around the wall blocking his view from the front door. The alarm panel installed beside the door had gone dark, which meant no contacting his team, local police, the feds. Nobody. They were on their own. "They cut the power from the backup generator. Whole system's down."

"I counted three exits when we got here. Front door, back door and that side door across the living room. Not to mention the windows." Her fingers slipped over his arm as though the mere contact with him could steady the frantic tone in her voice. She studied the wide expanse of open field between the house and the tree line to the west. "They can't cover them all. We could get to those trees without them knowing we left the house. Make a run for it."

"I'm not taking the chance they didn't come alone." His gaze dipped to the slight bulge along her lower abdominals. The stakes were too high. Dropping the magazine out of his weapon, he counted three rounds left after the shoot-out at the cabin and slammed it back into place. He'd left his extra ammunition in his SUV back at her aunt's cabin, and the rounds Raleigh had buried in backpacks all over that forest didn't fit his weapon. Damn it. There were too many windows in this place, too many sight lines and not enough bullets to keep Raleigh safe. For all they knew, whoever'd stolen that money from Mothers Come First could've contracted the job to tie up loose ends out to a professional. "Get behind me and stay there. Anything happens, use me as a shield."

She did as he asked, the spot where her fingers had held on to him still warm. Her exhalation brushed against the back of his neck as she lowered her voice. "Please tell me you have a plan to get us out of here."

"The previous owner had a car in the garage when we seized the property." Beckett scanned the property through the wall of windows on the other side of the house, heart in his throat. He slid his phone from his pocket and handed it to her. "I'm going to get you to it. Then I want you to get as far from here as you can. Lie low until I can come for you. Understand? If I don't make it out, don't come back here."

"I told you," she said. "I'm not leaving you here to fight alone."

"You're pregnant with my baby, Raleigh. I think I'm entitled to put your safety first—" Movement caught his attention from one of the windows. Beckett twisted around and lunged, colliding with her. "Get down!"

They hit the floor hard as another bullet ripped past overhead. Adrenaline dumped into his veins, and the pain in his shoulder dimmed. Hauling her into his chest with his uninjured arm, he got them both to their feet and pulled her into the hallway for cover. He raised the gun and took aim around the smooth corner of the wall, firing once. Twice. Glass shattered onto the hardwood floor, but Beckett wasn't going to stick around to see if he'd hit the target. Raleigh was the priority. Getting her to that vehicle was the priority. "Go!"

Light gray walls and unfamiliar artwork blurred in his vision as they raced past the small home office and bedrooms branching off the hallway. Blood trickled along the inside of his arm, coating his palm. Wouldn't take long for the shooter to figure out where they'd gone. All they had to do was follow the trail Beckett was leaving behind, but he'd be waiting for them. One bullet. That was all it would take to keep Raleigh safe.

She wrenched the garage door open and disappeared inside mere steps ahead of him.

Darkness enveloped them as Beckett charged through the door. He couldn't see a damn thing with the automatic lights out of commission. Raleigh's heavy breathing cut through his senses, and he reached out for her. Soft, damp hair slipped through his hand, triggering his heart rate to slow slightly. They made their way to the front of the garage. The faster he got her away from here, the sooner she'd be safe. That was all that mattered. "We'll have to open the door manually."

"We'll be giving up our position if we do that," she said. "We can still make it to the trees."

His heart beat hard behind his ears, but through that dull sound gravel crunched beneath heavy footsteps outside the garage door. Her outline took shape beside him as his eyes slowly adjusted to the darkness. Beckett pulled her flat against him and lowered his mouth to her ear. "They already know we're here."

And seeing as how the shooter had tracked them here so quickly, it looked like they weren't going to stop until they got what they'd come for. Raleigh.

He shifted his weight between both feet, tension tightening the tendons between his neck and shoulders. Pain slithered across his back and down his left arm as he held on to her. "Get in the car. Last time I checked, the keys were in the middle console. The second I get that door open, I want you to floor it as hard as you can." He felt more than saw the hesitation in the hardness of the muscles along her arm. "You went into hiding to protect our baby. I'm going to need you to do that again. Promise me you'll get as far from here as possible."

She nodded. "I promise."

The sound of footsteps died. One second. Two. Raleigh slipped into the luxury car and started the ignition as Beckett reached for the small red manual release attached to the garage door. The moment he opened this door, they'd be exposed. Vulnerable. Fumes built inside the enclosed space and burned down his throat, but he wasn't going to make the first move. He adjusted his grip on the gun. He had one shot left. What was their attacker waiting for?

Gunfire tore through the metal door, white streaks of light piercing through the small holes. A click registered. The shooter was reloading. Beckett pulled the release, and the garage flooded with sunlight as the door shot up the track. "Now!"

The car shot backward, barely missing the single masked shooter dressed in head-to-toe black, and spun around toward the dirt road leaving the property. The shooter had reloaded and took aim at the car, but Beckett was already running. He collided with a wall of lean muscle, the bullet in his shoulder screaming in protest. The shooter's weapon slid into the dirt, out of reach, as Beckett fought for control. Sunlight glinted off metal as he shoved to his feet. He dodged the first swing of the assailant's blade, then the second. He struck out, bone meeting flesh, and the suspect stumbled back. The shooter raised his weapon to take the final shot. Raleigh had almost made it to the fence, but the car was crawling to a stop. No. *No, no, no, no.* She had to keep going. She had to get out of here.

His opponent recovered fast. Charging with the knife in one hand, his attacker went for the soft tissue in Beckett's gut. He managed to dodge the fatal strike to his organs, but Beckett wasn't fast enough to block the next move with his injured shoulder.

The blade sank deep into his right thigh. A scream lodged in his throat as the shooter hit him in the left kidney, then the right, and his gun discharged. Lightning struck behind his eyes a split second before he hit the ground. The bastard followed through with a kick to his ribs. The sickening crunch of bone crushed the air from his lungs. He couldn't breathe, couldn't think. He strained to get a visual on the car. On Raleigh.

Fire engulfed the sky.

The explosion rocked through him, a wall of dust fleeing in the wake of red-and-orange flames shooting into the air, and his entire world shattered. "Raleigh!"

Grip on the knife in Beckett's leg, the shooter stood above him and pulled the weapon free. Then wiped it clean with one sleeve. "None of this would've had to happen, Marshal Foster, if Raleigh would've just taken the fall like she was supposed to."

Not a man's voice. Who the hell had come after…? Beckett struggled to hang on to consciousness, but he'd lost too much blood. He couldn't keep his eyes open, and he fell into blackness.

TWIGS AND THORNS tore at her skin as Raleigh rolled into the bushes. Heat—so much heat—seared over her exposed skin. She raised her hand in front of her face to block the burn, but there was nothing left to see. Flames consumed the dry brush around her from the pile of twisted metal. The car had been wired to explode. If she hadn't gotten out once she'd realized the electrical system was failing, she wouldn't have escaped in time.

She pushed her hair out of her face, the crisp edges of dried leaves tickling her palms in the strands. She turned back toward the house. The shooter. They must've gotten to the vehicle before she and Beckett had. How? The house's alarm system had been engaged before the power had gone off-line. Had they slipped inside before then or had they been waiting to make their move since Beckett had brought her here? She didn't know. Didn't care. She had to find Beckett, had to make sure he was okay.

Raleigh pushed to her feet and headed back toward the house. She'd made him a promise, but that'd been before her only means of escape had exploded. Now she had to go back. Breathtaking pain speared through her side as the adrenaline from the explosion drained. She tugged at the sweater she'd borrowed from the previous owner…and froze. Blood. A wave of dizziness flooded through her at the sight. A thin piece of jagged shrapnel, a quarter inch wide in some areas and a few inches long, protruded from her right side beneath the thick cables of yarn. She couldn't risk infection spreading to the baby. She had to remove the shrapnel and clean the wound. Raleigh struggled to breathe evenly through the pain, to stay on her feet.

Whoever had stolen that money didn't only want her dead. They were trying to destroy her completely. Who would do this to her? Who would risk shooting a US marshal for the chance of making sure she never uncovered the truth?

She scanned the dirt road leading back toward the house and stumbled forward. Shifting her sweater over the wound, she spit to counteract the dirt stuck to the inside of her mouth. There was a first-aid kit in the house. She remembered seeing it in the garage. "Beckett."

Her throat burned as black smoke billowed into the sky and shadowed the ground in front of her. She forced one foot in front of the other until she reached the garage. No sign of Beckett or the… Her chest constricted. Drag marks carved into the dirt threatened to trip her as the weight of her upper body pulled her around the side of the house. Beckett. Crusted blood flaked in her palms from trying to slow his bleeding in the kitchen.

He had to be here. He had to be alive. She'd come back to her aunt's cabin in desperation, but having him here these past eighteen hours had forced her to confront the demons she'd been hiding from her whole life. One kiss. That was all it'd taken to replace the pain, the loneliness and isolation with something she hadn't felt in so long, hadn't believed was meant for her—even for those brief seconds. He'd given her a glimpse of hope.

And she wasn't leaving without him.

Dry dirt gave way to green grass as Raleigh followed the drag marks to the large barn across the property. Her legs threatened to collapse right from under her as she caught sight of one of the main doors partially slid back on its track. Hadn't it been closed when they'd arrived? Pressing her back against the opposite door, she twisted her head to see inside, instincts on high alert. Ice slid through her as she caught sight of the body in the middle of the floor. "Beckett!"

Dried grass crunched under her boots as she rushed inside and dropped beside him. His chest rose and fell in shallow rhythms. He was alive, but unconscious. Her hands hovered above the bloody stain spreading across his shirt from where he'd been shot in the shoulder, the tubing she'd tied still in place, but now there was a second wound in his thigh. She had to stop the bleeding. Applying pressure on his thigh, she pressed her weight into him. "It's going to be okay. I'm here. I'm here. Stay with me."

Pulling the phone he'd given her from her back pocket with her free hand, she noted a mere glance of her reflection in the cracked glass. The phone must've been destroyed when she'd rolled from the car. She couldn't call anybody. Tears burned in her eyes. She wasn't trained for this. She wasn't a doctor. Raleigh forced herself to take a deep breath. But neither of those things was going to stop her from trying to save his life. "Hold on a little bit longer. I'm going to get you out of here."

"You're not going anywhere." Another reflection in the shattered glass hiked her pulse into dangerous territory, and Raleigh lunged to the side. The phone slipped from her hand as she turned to confront her attacker, but a hand fisted the hair at the side of her head and thrust her into the floor. The world tilted on its axis as black shoes slipped into her vision. Crouching beside her, the masked shooter—maybe the same one from the cabin, she didn't know—gripped her chin in one hand. "I was hoping it didn't have to come to this, Raleigh, but you wouldn't follow the script we gave you. Like I told your marshal over there. None of this would've happened if you'd taken the fall for stealing the donations like you were supposed to."

Recognition flared as brown eyes settled on her, and something inside Raleigh broke. She'd been right all along, but knowing who'd betrayed her didn't make the truth any easier. The pain in her side intensified the deeper she breathed. "You can take the mask off, Emily. You, of all people, should have the guts to face me after what you've done."

"You always were too smart for your own good. I told my employer we should've gotten rid of you as soon as you started looking into those transfers, but they've always had a soft spot for you. Don't ask me why." A gun materialized in Emily Cline's hand as her former assistant pulled the thick ski mask over her head and tossed it a few feet away. Long black hair had been sleeked back in a low ponytail, accentuating the fullness of the woman's nose and lips. The same smile her assistant had greeted her with every morning Raleigh had walked into her office tugged at the corners of her mouth. Emily ran her free hand over the frizzed hair trying to escape, the gun still aimed directly at Raleigh. Thick arched eyebrows drew together to form three small lines as her former assistant used the barrel of her weapon to move a piece of hair out of Raleigh's face. "As far as I'm concerned, you were the perfect patsy, someone we could use and discard like so many others have done before. That's why we targeted you, Raleigh. All those foster families, your aunt. Even the marshal over there. You weren't good enough for any of them. Nothing you did could make them love you, and now you've outlived your use for us."

The words carved through her, just as Emily had meant them to. Heat rushed into Raleigh's face and neck, her heart rate spiking at the base of her throat. She diverted her gaze to the floor, not willing to let her attacker know exactly how deep she'd cut, but she couldn't keep her attention from straying to Beckett lying there, bleeding on the ground.

The fact she'd been rejected—betrayed—by so many had made her an easy target to Emily and whoever else had framed her for stealing those donation funds, and her heart tightened in her chest. Because Emily was right. Nothing she'd done had made any of those families want to keep her, made her aunt love her, and despite the fact she and Beckett had been together for six months, in the end, he'd walked away from her, too.

If it'd been as easy as her getting arrested to tear them apart, then what they'd had... It hadn't been real. At least, not for him, but that didn't change the fact Beckett was her baby's father, and she'd do whatever it took to make sure their daughter was loved by both of her parents as long as she could help it.

"From what it sounds like, you're just a fixer, Emily. You're not the brains behind the plan to embezzle from the foundation. You're a pawn, like me. So who's the one making the moves?" She dug the tips of her fingers into the barn floor, hay bending under her grip as Emily stared her down. Air pressurized in her lungs the longer her former assistant had the gun trained on her, but if there was a chance she could find out who Emily worked for—and stay alive in the process—she'd take it. She wasn't going to die here. "Do you really believe you won't outlive your use to whoever you're working for when all of this is over? That they'll protect you when the truth comes out?"

A low laugh escaped Emily's throat as she shook her head and straightened. Lowering her voice, the shooter leaned in as though she were about to tell Raleigh a secret. "Everything that's happened these past few months—the forged signatures on the transfers, the offshore accounts in your name and the shell companies—that was all me. My plan, my execution. Only now I wish I would've killed you sooner. Would've saved me a whole hell of a lot of trouble."

Emily aimed the gun at Raleigh's chest, and every cell in Raleigh's body screamed in warning. She couldn't stop a bullet, but she wasn't going to go down without a fight either. Beckett was losing blood. Fast. Pressing her heels into the floor, she ignored the pain tearing through her side where the shrapnel shifted beneath her sweater and prepared to rush her former assistant as fast as she could.

Movement registered from behind the shooter, and she realized Beckett was conscious. She kept her gaze on Emily as he fought to get to his feet. Was he going to attack from behind? He'd already taken a bullet to the shoulder and what looked like a knife wound to his thigh. How much more blood could he lose before his body started shutting down? Her mouth dried. Desperation clawed up her throat. They had to get out of here, but without Emily in cuffs, the shooter would keep coming after them, and they wouldn't have any proof to clear Raleigh's name. Raleigh had to give Beckett a chance. Before Emily realized he'd gotten to his feet. "If you kill me, the secondary account you and your partner have been hiding from the FBI will be exposed."

Emily kept her expression hard as stone aside from the slight downturn of one corner of her mouth. A piece of straw snapped under Beckett's boot, and the shooter twisted around, finger on the trigger.

And fired.

Chapter Seven

"No!" Long dark hair and a flash of red against white blurred in front of him as Raleigh tackled the shooter to the ground. She was alive. The explosion… She must've gotten free of the blast, but now the shooter who'd tried to kill her was scrambling for the gun.

The bullet burned across the surface of his arm but missed puncturing another hole in his body. Beckett stumbled forward, dizzy. Every nerve ending in his leg screamed for relief. The attacker's knife hadn't gone too deep, but there was a possibility he was losing blood a lot faster than he'd originally calculated. He closed in on the two women struggling for the weapon.

That flash of red along Raleigh's white T-shirt. A sickening twist knotted his gut. She could've been injured in the explosion. He had to get her out of here. Had to get her help. What if it affected the baby? Neither of them would forgive themself if something happened to their daughter. His injured leg dragged behind him, and a single kick from the attacker knocked him off-balance. He hit the ground, his shoulder reminding him there was still a piece of steel lodged deep in the muscles of his shoulder.

Wrapping her gloved hands around Raleigh's throat, the woman she'd called Emily fought to smother his future right in front of him. Raleigh's legs kicked out in an attempt to loosen the other woman's grip, but the shooter had the advantage, and she knew it.

"Get your damn hands off of her." A growl built in his chest as he reached out for the nearest item he could use as a weapon—a shovel—and swung. Hard. The metal reverberated off bone into his hands, and the shooter collapsed onto her side. Strained coughing kicked his heart rate into overdrive as Raleigh struggled to sit upright, and he tossed the shovel. Crouching beside Raleigh, he skimmed the angry red skin along her neck. "Tell me you're okay. Is the baby okay?"

"I think so." Her hand shook above her wound as she pulled the oversize green sweater away. She nodded, out of breath. Wild green eyes focused on the woman unconscious beside her. "It was her. Emily. She pretended to be my assistant so she could ensure all the evidence of the missing funds pointed to me like we thought. She set up the offshore accounts in my name, forged my signature on the transfers. All of it, but she wasn't working alone."

"She had a partner." Clarity slid through him for the first time since he'd caught up to her in that old cabin less than twenty-four hours ago. Hell. Had it really only been a day? Beckett pulled a set of cuffs—the same set he'd secured Raleigh with— and dragged Emily's wrists behind her back. Slight movements from the hay in front of her mouth said she was still alive, but she'd have to deal with a hell of a headache when she woke. "Makes sense. My guess is she's a professional. She's been trained in weapons and hand-to-hand combat better than most of the deputies on my team. Someone like that is usually only good for one thing—following orders. She was hired. Emily probably isn't even her real name. Most likely a cover planted inside the foundation."

He hauled Emily from the floor and dragged her upright against one of the empty horse stalls, his leg threatening to give out with each step. Sweeping the shooter's gun from the floor, he tucked it into his empty shoulder holster. Where his service weapon had ended up, he had no idea. Right now, it didn't matter. He'd just make damn sure Emily never laid another hand on Raleigh again. Ever.

"Whoever sent her to kill us is going to know she didn't finish the job. If they were willing to hire someone like this in the first place, there's nothing stopping them from doing it again." Raleigh wedged her boots into the hay-covered floor until her back pressed against the opposite stall from Emily. Clutching her side with one hand, she slid her palm across her lower abdominals with the other, as though seeking assurance the small life inside was still there after nearly being blown to pieces. Fresh blood spread beyond the border of where her sweater skimmed the waistband of her jeans. Color drained from her face as she shook her head slowly. "We're still in danger. We'll always be in danger as long as I'm a loose end. It's never going to stop."

"I'm going to find who did this. I give you my word. I'm not going to let anyone hurt you again. Understand?" Crouching as best he could in front of her, he swept her sweater out of the way, one hand cradled at her lower back as he studied the piece of shrapnel in her side. Shallow exhalations brushed against the overheated skin of his neck despite the frigid temperatures outside. Ripping his coat from his shoulders, he bit down on the groan working up his throat from the bullet wound. "You're losing blood. Stay as still as you can while I find something to get that metal out."

"This wasn't how I imagined seeing you again." Her lashes brushed against the tops of her cheeks. Letting her hand fall to the top of her thigh, she revealed the bloodstained handprint across the white T-shirt she wore. Directly over where their baby would be.

"How exactly did you think it would play out?" He had to keep her talking, had to get her to hang on. Because despite the mess they'd made of their relationship, he still gave a damn about what happened to her. Her and their baby. Beckett shoved to his feet. He pushed the pain and weakness in his leg to the back of his mind. Red-and-white decals drove him toward the large first-aid kit hung against one wall of the barn. Clean her up. Get her to safety. Nothing else mattered.

His heart stalled in his chest as he turned at her lack of response and noted the slackness in her expression. He hauled the kit from the wall and limped back to her side. The kit skidded across the cement, bits of dust and hay digging into his knees. Framing one hand along her jawline, he brushed her hair out of the way with the other. She was breathing but unconscious. Sweat built in a thin layer along her temples. Couldn't be an infection. Not this fast. "Raleigh, open your eyes."

No answer.

No. He maneuvered her flat onto her back, raised his voice and checked her pulse at the base of her throat. "Raleigh."

"Looks like I've done my job after all." The thud of Emily Cline setting her head back against the warm-colored wood of the stall reached his ears. "Although I have to admit, Raleigh Wilde wasn't nearly as easy to surprise as her partner, but this was a lot more fun. A challenge."

"Calvin Dailey." Of course Emily had killed him. Because the only person who could clear Raleigh's name couldn't be left to the chance he'd never talk to the feds in the future. Beckett didn't bother looking at the woman sent to ruin Raleigh's life as he spun the first-aid kit latch toward him. He riffled through the contents, pulling alcohol, cotton pads and an emergency sewing kit from inside. "Say another word, and I'll make sure you don't wake up a second time."

"Promises, promises, Marshal Foster." Emily Cline's laugh pooled dread at the base of his spine. "But don't forget, I was able to insert myself into a global foundation and operate without raising any red flags from the executives for over a year, and the only way I could've done that was by doing my research. I know you." The weight of her attention constricted the air in his chest. "Your moral code you pride yourself on so highly doesn't let you see in anything but black and white since you realized your father was the reason you lost your mother. At least, until yesterday, when you decided that woman was worth risking your career and everything you believed in. You're finally seeing the world isn't black-and-white. No matter how many criminals you've put away to prove otherwise, I know you won't kill me in cold blood. You don't have it in you."

Beckett's hands hovered above Raleigh's wound, blood trickling from the shrapnel with every shallow breath she took. His ears rang at the sight. He couldn't breathe. Couldn't see anything in front of him but the dark outline of his mother bleeding to death on the floor of their farmhouse all those years ago. His vision swam, his heart pounding hard behind his ears to the point he thought he might pass out. The only person who'd ever supported him, who'd always been there for him, had slipped away as easily as water draining from a tub.

No. Not the only person. Beckett forced himself back into the moment. If it hadn't been for Emily Cline and whoever else was involved in embezzling that money from the foundation, Raleigh wouldn't have been arrested, wouldn't have left him. He hadn't been able to help his mom then. It'd been too late for her, but it wasn't too late for Raleigh. Beckett raised his gaze to the woman merely hired to take everything that he cared about from him. "You don't know a damn thing about me or what I'm capable of."

"The problem isn't me knowing what you're capable of, Marshal. It's how little you know about me." The cuffs rattled as Emily leaned forward, stretching her arms straight behind her. She wound her legs beneath her and brought her cuffed wrists to the front. In less time than it'd taken to put her in the cuffs, she was suddenly standing. She moved fast, diving forward for the gun he'd set down a few feet away while trying to take care of Raleigh's injury.

Beckett lunged, but he wasn't fast enough. Hand

gripped around steel, he bit back the scream of pain as Emily's boot crushed down hard on the wound in his shoulder. In less than a few seconds, he found himself at the wrong end of the gun.

"I'm sure you can understand the kind of pressure I'm under to finish this job, Marshal Foster. So forgive me if I'm not willing to let you save her life first." The shooter increased the pressure on his shoulder. "You're unarmed. You don't have a vehicle or any way to contact your team out here. You can chase me if you want. I might even enjoy it, but that means arresting your suspect or leaving Raleigh here to bleed out. What's it going to be? Uphold the oath you made as a deputy or break that legendary moral code of yours to save a fugitive?"

Blood pooled beneath one side of Raleigh's body. She was running out of time, but bringing Emily Cline in would clear her name of the embezzlement charges and give their baby the future he and Raleigh both wanted. Beckett tried pulling his arm out from under the weight of the shooter's foot, but the pain limited the use of the muscles across his back and down his arm. Twisting his head up, he locked his attention on his attacker. If he went after Emily, he wouldn't have a future. Period. But if he let Emily slip away, Raleigh would spend the rest of her life looking over her shoulder. And so would their daughter.

Not happening.

Beckett rolled out from under her boot and swung

a hard right toward her jaw. Emily dodged the hit, and his momentum pulled him forward. Agony tore down his spine as the shooter cracked the butt of her weapon at the base of his skull. He went down beside Raleigh, dirt filling his mouth and lungs. His hand pressed against hers as Emily stood above him. His body wouldn't obey his commands. Raleigh. He had to get up. "Stay away from her."

The shooter's weak smile broke through the darkness as she crouched next to him, dark hair sliding into her face, but her brown eyes didn't reflect the coldness visible a few minutes ago any longer. "We all have our roles to play, Marshal. This is mine."

UNCONSCIOUSNESS RIPPED OUT from under her as throbbing tore through her side. Sunlight speared her retinas, blinding her until the outline of someone in front of her took shape. She pressed her feet into the floor to stand, but something kept her pinned in the chair she'd been set into. Rope? Raleigh tugged at her wrists, the bark scratches along her forearms still stinging. Not rope. The edges of the material were too sharp. Zip ties. She blinked against the wide spread of blood across her T-shirt. The piece of shrapnel had been removed, but she was still bleeding. Her throat burned as she cleared a coat of dirt layering her mouth and raised her head from her chest. "Beckett?"

"I'm afraid he won't be able to save you this time." The dark shape in front of her shifted. Her eyes adjusted slowly, but she didn't need to see who'd tied her to the chair against one of the horse stalls to recognize that voice. "Unfortunately for him, he won't be saving anyone when this is over."

"Emily. What are you…?" Dizziness flooded through her, blurring the fine lines around the woman's wide brown eyes. Nausea churned in her stomach. The baby. She hadn't eaten in a few hours and her blood sugar had dipped. Raleigh shook her head to clear the tension working down her spine. "What did you do to him?"

"Nothing a surgeon can't fix, and as long as you're straight with me, I can get him to a hospital in time." Emily gripped a pair of rounded pliers typically used in shoeing horses and clenched between the teeth a jagged piece of shrapnel. The same piece of shrapnel that'd been embedded in Raleigh's side. Her former assistant had removed the sliver, and the blood trickling down Raleigh's side flowed more freely. She discarded the pliers and the jagged metal onto the floor. "But you don't have long at all."

She was bleeding out.

"What do you want?" She pulled her inner wrists apart, but there wasn't any room to maneuver. Emily had made sure of that.

"Who else aside from Marshal Foster and Calvin Dailey did you tell about what you found during your little off-the-books investigation?" Sunlight reflected off a long piece of steel as Emily pulled a blade from her back.

What she'd found? She hadn't found anything in the four months she'd been looking for whoever'd set her up to take the fall for the embezzlement charges. All she had was a theory with no proof to back it up. What she had found, she was sure the feds had already combed through. The offshore accounts and wire transfers, it all pointed to her. That was the entire point of Emily's and her partner's operation, wasn't it? "I'm not telling you anything until I know Beckett is safe."

A low-pitched laugh blustered from between the shooter's lips. Raleigh eyed the heavy metal pliers her former assistant had forgotten about.

"Every second you waste here is another second your marshal doesn't have, and I'm starting to lose my patience with you, Raleigh." Emily stood, the blade gripped tight in one hand. She shifted her weight between both feet as though forcing herself not to end this interrogation prematurely. Which, if she were being honest with herself, Raleigh appreciated. "Who else knows about the secondary account, the one the feds haven't linked to the missing donations? I recovered the hidden file on your laptop you stashed in the safe at the cabin. I know you found it, and Marshal Foster is running out of time."

Raleigh had threatened to expose the account in an attempt to make Emily reconsider spilling more blood, but it'd been mostly bravado at the time. She'd taken a shot in the dark after calculating how much money had been taken from the accounts she'd overseen for the foundation and the amount the FBI had reported missing during their investigation. The numbers didn't match up, which meant Emily and whoever else she was working for hadn't funneled everything into one account. There had to be another or maybe several, and the feds had no idea they existed.

"Either I see Beckett or you risk going back to your boss empty-handed with a whole lot of blood leading back to you." She was taking a risk making demands. The back of her neck prickled, and she stretched her hands to work out a cramp along one tendon. A sharp, slightly rounded edge caught on her heated skin. The head of a nail? She slipped her thumb around the metal. If she could get her wrists closer to the stall door, she might be able to break the zip tie without Emily noticing. She just had to keep her former assistant distracted long enough to come up with a plan to get Beckett out of here. "I don't think you want that. You've accounted for everything in your operation. You've been planning this for a long time, and there's a lot of money at stake. How is it going to look to your employer when you fail? Do you think they'll let you walk away?"

"If I were you, I'd worry about yourself. Because when this is over, I'm going to enjoy watching the life drain from your eyes." Emily closed the distance between them and pressed cold steel against her throat.

The tip of the knife cut into the oversensitized skin below Raleigh's jaw, but she refused to flinch. Refused to give up an ounce of confidence.

"Funny, here I was thinking the exact same thing." Raleigh tried to relax the muscles down her back, but the pain in her side stole the air from her lungs. Unsticking her hair from her face with one shoulder, she followed Emily's path into one of the other stalls.

Her former assistant slid the stall door back on its rails, exposing the man unconscious in the hay. Emily locked dark brown eyes on her from less than ten feet away, and Raleigh's gut clenched. Beckett. "You know, I started watching you—studying you— long before I walked into your office that first day, Raleigh. I know you. I know what drives you, what scares you, even how far you're willing to go to protect the people you care about."

"I didn't realize this was a therapy session." Raleigh straightened her arms a bit more, then set the edge of the zip tie around her wrists on top of the partially exposed nail head behind her. Interlocking her fingers together, she applied as much pressure as she dared without giving away her attempt to escape. "Is this where you tell me all the reasons I keep people at arm's length or what my dreams really mean?"

"Not at all. It means I can pretty much do anything to you physically, mentally, emotionally, and nothing will get beneath that guarded exterior of yours. I could threaten and torture you all day, and I might get lucky, but neither of us has the time for that, do we? Quite admirable, in fact. Some of the best operators I've known can't withstand pain as long as you can, but Marshal Foster, on the other hand?" Emily sidestepped out from in front of the stall door where Beckett lay and unholstered the gun from beneath the black jacket she wore. She took aim at Beckett, and ice flooded through Raleigh's veins, straight to her heart. "Do you think he'll last long? I mean, I've already shot him and stabbed him, but how long do you think he'll hold on if I put another bullet in him? Should we see?"

The zip tie slipped from the nail behind her back as Raleigh turned her attention to the man who'd risked his life to protect her and their baby. "He has nothing to do with this. You know that."

"You brought him into this when you reached out to him after your arrest. You made him part of this." Emily raised her voice and slipped her finger over the trigger of the gun. "Now you have five seconds to tell me who else knows about that account before I put another bullet in him and make you watch him die before I kill you for good measure. Five…"

Raleigh increased the pressure against the zip tie around her wrists. "The second account is yours, isn't it? The one whoever hired you promised you'd walk away with after this was all over?"

"Four…" Emily readjusted her grip on the weapon.

"You don't have to do this," she said. "Please."

Her former assistant turned to Beckett. "Three, Raleigh. You're running out of time."

Raleigh lifted her wrists above the nail before slamming her hands down onto the nail. The zip tie snapped, and she rushed forward. Catching Emily around the middle, she tackled the shooter to the floor. A gunshot exploded loud in her ears, but she couldn't focus on that right now. Pure adrenaline and desperation burned through her. Fisting Emily's jacket by the collar, she slammed the gunwoman back into the cement as hard as she could.

Her attacker stopped fighting, Emily's brown eyes wide. The lines around her mouth and eyes softened with unconsciousness. The air rushed from Raleigh's lungs as she loosened her grip on the woman beneath her. Her fingers ached with the amount of force she'd used, just as they had all those years ago. She could still feel the edges of the rock digging into her hand as she'd brought it down against her aunt's head that day. Staring at the blood crusted in her palms, she pushed away from Emily. Raleigh fell back, barely able to keep herself upright. Whether from the blood loss or the rush of memories clouding her focus now, she didn't know, but she couldn't wait for Emily to come around. Her former assistant had been right. There wasn't anything she wasn't willing to do to protect the people she cared about.

They had to get out of here. She had to get Beckett help.

"Beckett." Her hands shook as she got to her feet and reached for him. "Come on. You have to get up. We need to get out of here."

A groan rumbled through his chest, and Raleigh couldn't stop the burst of relief escaping as she battled the burn of tears. Because if she didn't have this small release, she feared she might shatter right here on the floor. He was going to make it. She had to believe that, but first, she had to get him on his feet. "I'm going to help you stand, okay? We can do this."

She collected Emily's gun from where her former assistant had dropped it. Maneuvering his uninjured arm across her back, she ducked her shoulder beneath his side and forced his upper body up. Panicked seconds ticked by as she used the last of her remaining strength to get him to his feet and wedged him against her side. Her pain receptors caught fire as they headed for the main door. Emily hadn't moved. Hadn't given any sign she'd be regaining consciousness, but Raleigh wasn't willing to wait around for that to happen. The shooter wouldn't have walked here in case she had to make a quick getaway. Emily had to have a vehicle nearby, possibly hidden. She and Beckett just had to find it.

Before either of them collapsed from blood loss.

Chapter Eight

"Raleigh." Her name slipped past his lips as they stumbled from the stall into the main part of the barn together. His head hurt. Hell, his whole body hurt, but it was nothing compared to the sight of so much blood spreading across her shirt. "Stop. You need—"

"We need to keep moving." Her fingers fisted tight in his shirt as she struggled to take most of his weight. How she was able to keep walking and drag his injured butt at the same time, he had no idea. Seemed no matter the circumstance, she was determined to prove how strong she could be, but Raleigh didn't need to prove anything to him. She never had. Well, other than her innocence. "She's not going to be out for long."

Emily Cline. Damn it. She was right. They had to get out of here. The woman had been sent to tie up loose ends, to make sure Raleigh never got the chance to clear her name, and she wouldn't stop until the job was done. As much as Raleigh's former assistant had researched him, he knew her kind, too, and he wasn't going to wait around to see how far the shooter would go to complete her mission. They'd lost this battle, but he sure as hell would find out who was behind this war. He'd do whatever it took, for however long it took, to take them down.

"I've got you. Keep your weight on me." Raleigh led them through the main barn door and out into the open. The toe of his boot dragged behind him as the stab wound weakened his right leg, but she didn't show any signs of slowing despite her uneven exhalations. Keeping her gaze dead ahead, she directed them toward the nearest spread of pines to the west. "We're going to make it. I promise. We just need to retrace Emily's footprints back to her vehicle, okay?"

He'd been an idiot. Even if Emily hadn't caught up with their trail, how the hell had he ever convinced himself Raleigh had taken that money? Every sacrifice she'd made was for the people she cared about. She hadn't reached for his backup weapon at her aunt's cabin to make another run for freedom but to give them a chance of survival during the shoot-out. She could've disappeared in the middle of the night when they'd made camp, but instead she'd soothed him when the nightmares came for him. Then she'd offered to turn herself in to keep him and their baby safe. Criminals didn't do that.

The evidence had been all right there, perfectly staged and easily accessible to anyone who'd come to investigate the missing donation funds, made it look like she'd turned into the kind of criminal he hated the most, the kind that hurt others to gain for themselves. The kind of criminal like his father, a man who didn't give a damn about the consequences of his selfishness. But that wasn't Raleigh. Never had been. Everything she'd done had been for the benefit of others, especially their unborn baby. "I trust you."

He meant it, too. They were going to make it. Because Raleigh Wilde never looked a challenge in the face and backed down, and he couldn't help but admire her for that. When it'd come right down to it, he'd been a coward when he'd cut her out of his life after her arrest. He hadn't wanted to feel the pain of losing another person he'd given a damn about to the wrong side of the law, so he'd convinced himself he hadn't known her at all, hadn't loved her. Hadn't been compromised in any way, but it'd all been a lie.

Her grip strengthened around his arm draped along her shoulders. "Is it too soon to remind you I suggested we make a run for the trees when the first bullet went through the window?"

"You can say I-told-you-so as much as you want after we get the hell out of here." He set his back teeth against the throbbing ripping through his shoulder with each swing of his arm. There was only twenty feet left between them and the tree line. As soon as they reached cover, he'd take a look at her wound. From the amount of blood plastering her sweater to the shirt beneath, he figured she had maybe ten—fifteen—minutes at the most before she collapsed. She was one of the most ambitious, driven and impressive women he'd ever known, and that included the chief deputy of his division. Then again, she could only push herself while pregnant for so long before all that fire ran out. This woman was nothing like he'd come across before, but that didn't make her immune to the things the rest of the mere mortals on earth physically succumbed to. Infection, blood loss, exhaustion. "We need to get you to the hospital."

Ten feet until they'd reach the trees. Green grass bled to dying wildflowers and slightly cooler temperatures in the shade of the pines.

"I…can't. I'm still a fugitive, Beckett. If I go there…they'll take me into custody." Her hand slipped from his waist. Color drained from the patches of red along her face and neck, those mesmerizing green eyes suddenly distant. Her breathing changed, growing more shallow, uneven. She stumbled forward.

Beckett caught her a split second before she collapsed, but her weight and the lack of strength in his right leg pulled him down along with her. Gravel cut into his palms as he braced himself from landing on top of her. She was still conscious. Barely. He scanned the rest of the property for any sign Emily had followed their trail. They couldn't wait for her to catch up. A scream built in his chest as he worked his uninjured arm under her lower back and hauled her up over his shoulder in a fireman's hold. His leg throbbed. She was right. She was on the FBI's most wanted list. They couldn't walk right into a public hospital without alerting local PD and the feds. She'd be taken back into custody, and he'd have to answer for not bringing her in. "I've got someone who can help. A former combat medic. He's a marshal. I trust him."

But could they take the risk?

"Then that'll have…to be good enough for me," she said. "I can walk. You're still…bleeding."

Pressure should've released from behind his sternum as they crossed the tree line. They weren't out of the woods yet, metaphorically speaking, but they at least had a chance to disappear, to find cover. He should've been there for her after the arrest. He should've known better than to believe she'd taken that money, especially after showing him that first sonogram of the life they'd created together. He'd promised to always be there for her, no matter the circumstances, because that was what she'd needed. Someone she could trust, rely on, someone who cared about her after she'd been discarded by so many others, but he'd run at the first sign of trouble. "You might be out to prove to the world how strong and resilient you are, but that doesn't mean you don't need someone to take care of you every now and then."

Beckett adjusted his grip at the back of her knees. He wouldn't run again.

"Not to the world." Her voice softened, somehow distant yet reverberating down his spine at the same time. "Just…you."

"You don't have to prove anything to me." He was the one who'd betrayed her, but he'd spend the rest of his life making it up to her if that was what it took. Beckett pushed deeper into the woods, that knot of uncertainty growing bigger in his gut. It wouldn't take much for the shooter to catch up with them, considering the amount of blood he was leaving behind on his own and the fact Emily wasn't carrying another person on her back, but he wasn't going to stop following the shooter's prints in the mud. Not until Raleigh was safe.

Up ahead, sunlight glinted off tinted glass, and Beckett slowed. A dark SUV had been parked in the thickest part of the woods to cover Emily's approach to the ranch, and he'd never been more thankful at the sight of a standard black vehicle in all his life. "Almost there. Just hang on. I'll get you out of here."

Silence descended around them. Moss-covered pines towered overhead, blocking sunlight from reaching the forest floor in some spots, and the hairs on the back of his neck rose on end. Damp wood and earth tickled his senses. Something was wrong. Well, other than they were fifty miles from the nearest hospital. Hell, from the nearest town.

Cold metal pressed to the back of his neck, and Beckett froze, air stuck in his lungs.

"I'm not leaving without her, Marshal." Emily's voice shook, but the barrel of a gun pressed to the base of his skull remained steady. She must've had a backup neither him nor Raleigh had noticed. One wrong move, and she'd pull the trigger.

Raleigh didn't have that kind of time. Neither of them did.

"You're already looking at the entire US Marshals Service coming down as hard as they can for attempted murder of a federal agent, Emily." His head throbbed, his pulse loud behind his ears. He didn't have a weapon and happened to be holding the one thing she wanted that he wasn't willing to give up—Raleigh. "You can end this now. All you have to do is let me get her to a hospital, and I can put in a good word with the district attorney after you turn yourself in and admit your part in all of this."

"You're right." Emily cocked the gun. "I can end this now."

Beckett tightened his hold on the woman in his arms and launched himself off to the right. The gun went off next to his ear. High-pitched ringing threw him off-balance, but he caught himself before letting Raleigh hit the ground. Rolling, he released his grip on her and shot to his feet before Emily could target him again. He wrapped one hand around her wrist and shoved to get the shooter as far from Raleigh as he could. One strike to her midsection. Two. He positioned her arm over his shoulder, hauled her over his back and slammed her onto the ground.

The rush of her lungs emptying didn't slow her for long. Swinging the gun toward him, Emily shot to her feet with a rolling growl escaping her chest. "You're only making this harder on yourself, Marshal. On both of you."

"Go to hell." Beckett reached out, wrapped one hand around the gun barrel and crushed his knee against her wrist. The gun disappeared into the underlying brush. He dodged the left hook aimed at his face and blocked the second attempt as he backed low out of her reach, but his leg slowed him down. Her knee landed hard against his jaw, and he stumbled back.

"Been there. Only this time you and your fugitive are coming with me." Emily spread her stance, ready to charge.

Three distinct gunshots exploded from a few feet away.

Emily pulled up short, brown gaze wide. Dropping her chin to her chest, she let her mouth fall open as blood spread across her front before collapsing face-first into the dirt. Dead.

Beckett located the second shooter, and his gut twisted. "Raleigh."

She held a hand to her bleeding side, dark hair wild around her face. Exhaustion etched deep lines around compelling green eyes staring down at the woman she'd shot. She lowered the gun, expression smooth and distant. "She can't hurt us anymore."

HE FELL TO his hands and knees, one hand over the stab wound in his thigh.

"Beckett!" Raleigh rushed forward. She'd neutralized the threat by shooting Emily, but he was still in danger of going into shock. Soon he'd lose enough blood to cause his organs to start shutting down one by one. She had to get him out of here. Emily's SUV. It was the only chance they had. Sliding her free hand across his muscled back, she forced him to sit up, fire igniting along her side. "We need to get to the car. Come on."

Her head pounded, fatigue overwhelming, but she wasn't going to give up on him. Because he hadn't given up on her. He'd had the chance. He could've brought her in after he'd discovered her hiding at the cabin, but he hadn't. He'd chosen to help clear her name, even if it'd been for the sake of their baby. He'd made the choice to break that legendary code of his and given his word to a fugitive. Now it was her turn to help him.

Raleigh dragged him in to her side, letting out the scream of pain that'd been building since she'd escaped the fireball set to kill her, and found a small rush of release. Something real and raw she hadn't felt in years. One step toward the shooter's vehicle. Two.

"Raleigh, stop," he said.

"No." She stumbled, unable to keep hiding the pain, unable to ignore the hurt she'd shouldered all these years. It crashed down around her as she battled to get Beckett to the SUV. Tears burned as mountains of uncertainty, doubt and effort slipped from the dark crevices she'd held on to protect herself. She'd convinced herself everything she'd been through—all the trauma, the betrayal, the shame—had carved her into a strong, emotionally impenetrable woman who never faltered, never failed, never relented. Who'd learned to rely on no one but herself, but she was so tired of holding it all together, tired of being numb. Day by day, she'd systematically become a black hole of nothingness to everyone around her after the incident on that beach, most recently Beckett. Invisible, unknown, void of anything to the naked eye, but over the past eighteen hours the man at her side had forced her to face the light, to feel, and she couldn't hide anymore. "I'm not letting you die out here. She doesn't get to win. She doesn't get to have this control over us."

"Find…" he said. "Reed."

"Reed?" Emily's gun still in hand, she hefted Beckett against the hood of the passenger side and fumbled for the door. The truth of the matter was she wouldn't have survived the past few hours without Beckett. She owed him her life—hers and the baby's—and she'd never be able to pay that back, but she was going to try. She wrenched the door open and maneuvered him to sit against the front seat before hoisting his legs inside. "Stay awake, damn it."

Rounding the front of the SUV, she clutched on to the hood as a rush of pain gutted her from the inside. The bleeding in her side hadn't slowed, but she couldn't stop now. Not after everything they'd survived. She closed her eyes, nails digging into the vehicle's paint. "You can do this. You have to do this."

Because she couldn't lose him. Not again.

The pressure in her gut released after a few seconds, and she pushed one foot in front of the other until she reached the driver's-side door. After hauling herself into the seat, she set the gun between her and Beckett and pressed the ignition button.

The engine growled to life for a few moments, then cut out.

Raleigh hit the ignition a second time, one hand tight around the steering wheel. Her heart thudded hard in her chest. Seconds slipped away. She punched the start button again. "Come on."

Nothing.

She slammed the palm of her hand against the steering wheel. Emily had to have a safety feature in place that prevented anyone else from taking off with her vehicle. Every minute she wasted here was another minute Beckett didn't have. Her hands trembled as she pulled the release for the door and slid from the car. Using the SUV for balance, she slipped her hand along the cool metal until she reached the front of the vehicle a second time and hesitated as her fingers traced the edge of the hood. The metal didn't line up, as though the hood had been popped. Hope flooded through her as she inserted her hand between the hood and the SUV's main frame and lifted slightly. The hood released, and she dropped it back into place. She slid back behind the steering wheel and pushed the ignition button. "We're going to make it. Stay with me."

The engine growled to life, and everything inside her released. She pulled the vehicle out of Park and maneuvered beyond the patch of pines as best she could before aiming the SUV toward the main road. Dirt kicked up alongside the vehicle on either side of them as she sped away from the ranch, away from Emily. Beckett's head swung toward the passenger-side window, but she didn't need to see his face to know he was running out of time. His shirt and jeans were already soaked through, and there were only so many pints of blood he could lose before he hit the point of no return. Raleigh floored the accelerator, Oregon countryside blurring through the side windows. The nearest hospital was at least fifty miles from here, but Beckett had said he knew of a combat medic. Someone he trusted.

She slid one hand across her abdomen, patches of dried blood starching her borrowed sweater. Bringing Beckett to a former combat medic, a marshal— someone she didn't know—would expose her, put her at risk. Was that the Reed he'd been telling her to find? Raleigh slid her attention to the bloodied man in the passenger seat. She'd have to take the chance. She'd have to trust him. "This baby deserves to know her daddy, Beckett, so I'm not letting you off that easy. If you're not going to hang on for me, do it for her."

The shooter's phone slid from one side of the middle console to the other as Raleigh took the turn onto the national forest road 21. The cell Beckett had given her had been crushed when she'd jumped from the car before it'd exploded, but there was a chance she could recover the SIM card. Gravity pulled at every cell in her body. Her eyes were heavier than a few minutes before as adrenaline drained from her veins, but she couldn't stop. One hand on the wheel, she tugged his phone from her back pocket. The screen was broken, sharp edges digging into her skin, but from what she could tell, the side of the phone hadn't been damaged all that much. She might be able to save the data card. Eyes on the road, she carefully and slowly pried the small green chip free and replaced Emily's with Beckett's. The screen lit up, and something inside of her threatened to break.

It'd worked.

But… A pitiful moan of defeat escaped her mouth. Her thumb hovered above the ten-button configuration of numbers. The phone was asking for a password. Beckett's password. Neither the facial recognition nor the touch identification would work until he'd entered the six-digit code since she'd transferred the SIM card. Damn it. She had to think.

Most people used the same passwords across devices and accounts. There had to be a code he frequently used, something easy to remember. She just had to remember any instances she'd seen him use it. Only, if she entered the wrong code three times, his entire contact list, along with any other data on the phone, would be erased, and she'd have no idea how to reach the person he'd called Reed. If that was even his contact's real name. Locking her jaw against the pain, Raleigh tugged on the wheel as the road curved around. They'd almost reached the Paulina Lake Campground. From there, she could either head south on the national forest road 500 or keep heading west, but she had no idea where this Reed person was, where he lived, if he could help them at all, and she wouldn't know any of that until she was able to get into Beckett's contact list.

Her blood pressure spiked. He'd already lost too much blood. How much longer before his body decided to shut down for good? "Okay. Six digits. Birthday?"

Using her thumb, she punched in the numbers for his birthday into the phone, but the passcode reset. Wrong sequence. Too easy. She had two tries left before the phone locked her out permanently and erased all the data on the SIM card. The split off ahead was coming up too fast, and Raleigh pressed her foot onto the brake pedal. "Beckett, I need you to wake up. I can't get into the phone without your password."

No response.

"Come on!" She forced herself to breathe as the main sign for the campground slid into view. She'd have to stop. She'd have to risk a few more minutes Beckett didn't have. The gunshot wound in his shoulder, the injury to his thigh… This was all her fault. She'd brought him into this mess, and she had no idea if she was going to be able to get him out of it. "Okay. You can do this, Wilde. You can do this."

She tried his mother's birthday next, but the small bubbles at the top of the screen reset again.

Nausea swirled in her stomach. They weren't going to make it. At least, not to the former combat medic. She'd have to take him to a public hospital. She'd have to risk being arrested a second time, never seeing her daughter once the birth was over, but if it'd save his life, she'd do it. For him.

Her gaze slipped to his empty shoulder holster and a flash of memory lit across her mind. That was it. It had to be. His gun safe. He'd kept it under his side of the bed when they'd been together. It'd had an electronic lock with a six-digit passcode, which… She inhaled on a shaky breath. Which had been the day they'd met. Raleigh pulled the vehicle off to the side of the road, her heart in her throat. He wouldn't have kept the same digits. Not after everything that'd happened between them, but she didn't have a whole lot of other options either. Most people didn't change their passcodes over time. Too hard to remember when habit had already rewired the neural pathways in their brains, but that didn't mean his hatred for her—for what she'd been accused of— wouldn't break that habit. Her hand shook as she entered the date, her lungs fighting for a full breath.

The screen went black.

Chapter Nine

"Gotta hand it to you, Foster. When you're trying to piss someone off, you go for the knockout," a familiar voice said. "It's amazing you're still alive. Thanks to me."

Beckett slid back into consciousness breath by slow, agonizing breath. Waves of soft light cascaded over the pale wood paneling overhead, one side of his body cold from the floor-to-ceiling windows stretching along one wall. He shot upright on the modern sofa—the kind with angles rather than cushions—automatically searching the space as his nervous system vaulted into his fight-or-flight response. He'd recognized the voice, but the man perched in one of those ridiculous wicker satellite chairs looked as though he'd aged years in the span of only a few days. Or maybe Beckett was superimposing what he felt like over the marshal who'd obviously saved his life. But where did that leave Raleigh? If she'd brought him here, she'd put herself at risk for arrest. "Reed."

"Yes?" Finnick Reed, former combat medical specialist turned US marshal, clutched a bag of cookies in one hand, rooting through the contents until he found one good enough for his particular tastes. Blue eyes lightened with the help of the firelight dancing on the television screen built into the side of a kitchen island across the room. Despite everything he'd seen, everything he'd been through, the ex-soldier fit perfectly with the stainless-steel, modern feel of the cabin.

Beckett's head pounded as he settled back against the awkward, uncomfortable sofa. Stars peppered the night sky through the windows. How long had he been out? Bits and pieces filtered through the haze clouding his memories. The barn, Raleigh leading them into the woods. Emily Cline's eyes widening seconds before she hit the ground. All of it fought for his focus as he listened for movement throughout the rest of the house. No movement. No sign of her. He clutched the edges of the sofa, his clothing stiff with patches of blood. "Where's Raleigh?"

"You mean the fugitive you told to contact me to save your life so you could put not only your entire career with the Marshals on the line but mine, as well?" Reed dived his hand into the bag for another cookie, crumbs catching in the clean-cut beard around his jaw and mouth. "That Raleigh?"

Blistering rage exploded through him while the deputy sat there as if nothing in the world mattered but those damn cookies. "If you handed her over to the feds, I swear to spend the rest of my life—"

"Relax, Foster. You trusted me for a reason." Reed tossed the bag onto the coffee table between them, mouthing something that looked a whole lot like "wow" as he leaned forward. "She's on the bed upstairs asleep. The woman could barely stand on her own, let alone carry your sorry hide up those stairs by herself, but she stood by you until I gave her doctor's orders to rest after a transfusion of her own. You've only been unconscious for four hours." Reed motioned to the other end of the sofa, where the barest of impressions dipped in the cushion. "I hit my elbow on the doorjamb bringing your unconscious body inside my house, if you care to know."

"I don't." She'd stayed with him despite the shrapnel injury in her side. Always putting others first, even at the cost of her own life. Hell, if he hadn't sent her running, she wouldn't have even been near that car when it'd exploded. The shooter had done enough research to look into Beckett's background. He should've known Emily Cline had just as easy a way into the seized property records. Or her partner did. Beckett rubbed at his eyes as the throbbing in his head echoed behind his ears. "How is she?"

He couldn't ask about the baby. As much as he trusted the deputy, that information was Raleigh's to share, and he doubted she'd let her pregnancy slip. Especially to someone she didn't know.

"Not in cuffs," Reed said.

"You know what I meant." Aside from the jokes and the constant sarcasm, Finnick Reed had watched Beckett's back enough times to earn his trust. A groan worked through his chest as he shifted his position on the couch. His shirt and jeans had been ripped to expose the stained gauze over both wounds.

"She didn't lose as much blood as you did, but she wouldn't let me patch her until I was able to get your bleeding under control and your vitals stable. Studied every move I made until I sewed in the last stitch like she was waiting for me to make a mistake. Something tells me I don't want to know what would've happened if I had." Reed stretched. His vintage-wash T-shirt emblazoned with a superhero logo rode higher. As if Reed was some modern-day, real-life hero—to himself and any woman who happened to be passing through his life. Who wore a threadbare T-shirt with formal trousers? Finnick Reed. That was who. The deputy stood, making his way around the black glossy kitchen island toward the refrigerator. He pulled two water bottles from the shelves and retraced his steps to hand Beckett one. "Both of you are damn lucky I answered the phone, and that I happen to keep stores of blood in my freezer instead of tater tots. Drink up. The headache is only going to get worse."

Beckett didn't give a damn about his headache right then, but he took the water anyway. The cold penetrated through the plastic straight down to bone, kept him grounded. There were only two things that mattered right now. Raleigh and their baby, and the danger closing in on them both, but he couldn't risk moving them until Raleigh had a chance to recover from the fight with Emily Cline. Unscrewing the cap to the bottle, Beckett took a long swig. "You could've turned us both in, saved yourself a whole lot of trouble."

"Now, where's the fun in that?" A smile tugged at one corner of Reed's mouth, deepening the laugh lines on either side of a nose that'd been broken one too many times. "Gotta tell you, having a woman like that show up on my doorstep in the middle of the night, not my worst day. Could've done without the blood on my couch, though. Next time remember it's supposed to stay on the inside of your body."

"I'll try to keep that in mind." Beckett wiped a thin layer of crusted blood onto his jeans from his hand. Hell, they were ruined anyway. "Give us until sunrise. Nobody has to know we were ever here."

Reed set his water bottle on the coffee table, untouched. Overgrown light brown hair lost its shape as the former combat medic interlocked his fingers between his knees. "Is it worth your career, Foster? What you're doing here. Is it worth risking everything you believe in, and the people who've watched your back all these years? Because I read her file. I saw the prosecution's case. Everything—all the evidence—led back to her." The deputy pointed his index finger at him as he stood, his shadow cast-

ing across Beckett's knees. "So whatever you have
in mind, you better do it fast. The longer you wait
to bring her in, the worse it'll get. Not just for you.
For all of us."

Beckett twisted his grip around the water bottle,
the plastic cracking. He put most of his weight into
his uninjured leg, shoved to his feet and stretched
out one hand. "Thanks for the help, Reed."

"Glad there was still time I could." Reed shook
his hand, then headed for the front door. He pulled
a deep tan trench coat from off the rack near the
alarm panel and slid his arms into each sleeve. "You
owe me a new couch, and one keep-my-name-out-
of-a-crime-scene-report card."

Damn it. Emily Cline's body. Sooner or later,
he'd have to answer for that, considering the shooter
had taken his service weapon off him and Raleigh's
prints would be discovered on the weapon that
killed her former assistant. Their prints and DNA
were all over that ranch. It wouldn't be hard for fo-
rensics to place them at the scene, but it looked like
Reed had bought them some time. "You got it."

A burst of cold air slithered into the new holes
in his clothes as Reed closed the door behind him.
Within seconds, the growl of an outdated, muscled engine filled the cabin and headlights flashed.
Beckett didn't wait around to watch the deputy
make his way down the mountain through the windows. Not when every instinct he owned was beg-
ging him to search her out. He headed for the thick

black handrail off one side of the kitchen leading up to the next level. The same color of sleek wood paneling followed him up the stairs and rounded the wide expanse of the master bedroom. A large queen-size bed took up most of the space in the center of the room, a minimalistic rack with hangers off to one side. Matching nightstands with lamps, light carpet, modern art hanging above the bed tied in the modern but rustic theme, and in the center of it all, the woman who made it all disappear.

Raleigh lay on one side, faced away from him. Long damp hair spread across the dark gray pillowcase. The clothes she'd been wearing were discarded on the floor, spots of bright red blood so stark against the white fabric of her undershirt, and his gut clenched. She'd stayed with him, watched over him, as Reed had worked to keep him from bleeding out, even at the risk of injuring herself further. That drive of hers, the one that pushed her to be the best, to get the job done, that had built her into the woman he'd fallen in love with all those months ago, kept her from seeing the consequences of putting everyone but herself first. She could've died out there. They could've lost the baby, but she was the reason he was standing here. She was the reason he hadn't given up hope.

"Stop standing there and get in the bed." Her sleep-coated voice sent heat through his veins. She rolled onto her opposite shoulder, hypnotizing green eyes settling on him, and the past two days slid to the back of his mind.

"There's plenty of room on the floor." Exhaustion dug into his muscles as he slipped off his boots and tossed his destroyed pants onto the floor, her gaze following his every move. Pressure built behind his chest, but not the same kind as when they'd been facing off against a professional killer. No, this was something deeper, more exposing. They'd been through hell together, and he guessed that made them more alike than he'd originally believed.

"Your chivalry is going to tear your stitches." She maneuvered back onto her side, the outline of the same gauze and tape Reed patched him with visible through the oversize superhero T-shirt she'd donned. "Besides, we're adults. I think we can keep our hands to ourselves."

It wasn't her hands he was worried about. After everything they'd been through at the ranch, he wanted nothing more than to hold her against him, to make sure she was real and this wasn't some nightmare he couldn't wake up from. Medical tape pulled at the hairs across his thigh, stinging. He went for the folded clothes on the bottom shelf of the clothing rack. He and Reed weren't the same size, but close enough to make the two-people-one-bed situation a little less awkward. Pain arced through him as he shoved both feet into a pair of sweats meant for someone less bulky than he was and threaded his arms into another one of Reed's superhero tees. He approached the bed, locking on the exhausted, intelligent woman under the sheets. "Enjoying the show?"

"It's been so long since I've seen the show, I've got to enjoy it while I can get it." Her laugh lit up the parts of him that hurt the most as he slipped between the warm sheets. Within seconds, he'd forgotten all about the pain as Raleigh pressed her back against his chest, a perfect fit against him. "Don't move a muscle, Marshal Foster."

Beckett rested his cheek against the crown of her head and closed his eyes. "I'm not going anywhere."

SHE TRACED THE OUTLINE of the gauze taped to his shoulder through the soft T-shirt he'd borrowed. His chest rose and fell in easy rhythms as morning sunlight pierced through the edges of the curtains. Nothing like before when she'd found him unconscious in that barn fighting for breath. He was warm and rough, and she didn't dare stir for fear of ruining this perfect moment. They'd survived. Somehow. He'd protected her when every second leading up to right now she'd doubted his promise, doubted he would keep his word, but he'd been there. Made sure they'd made it off that ranch alive.

Grazing his split bottom lip with her thumb, she gave in to the explosive memories of that gut-wrenching kiss they'd shared before the bullets had started flying. She could still taste him. His underlying flavor of peppermint and wildness, but that

kiss had been more than pure physical desire. It'd
been a hit to the invisible barriers she'd been building all her life, the distance she'd put between her
and everyone around her. The cracks had started
spreading when they'd been together for those short
few months, but after her arrest they had filled with
a clear ice she hadn't let anyone break through.
Only now... Now for the first time, she felt herself
trying to break down that barrier, break through
the distrust and hurt. He might've originally de-
fended her as some part of that moral code of his or
out of obligation to their baby, but he'd still saved
her life. He'd still kept his word to be there for her,
even when he'd had the chance to leave her behind, and the numbness from that destructive black
hole inside that'd always felt unwanted—unloved—
eased a bit. Her insides warmed as she settled her
chin against his uninjured shoulder and studied the
movement behind his closed eyelids. "How long
have you been pretending to be asleep?"

Piercing blue eyes matched the smile tugging
at one corner of his mouth. He slid his hand over
hers, positioned directly over his heart. The rhythmic beat pulsed through her, ensured this wasn't
just some dream. He was here. He was real. "Who
says I'm pretending?"

"You never were a good liar." A laugh bubbled up her throat as she leveraged her elbow into
the mattress to see his face better, something that
seemed to come easier the longer he was around.

The stitches in her side stretched but stayed in place. "So do you make it a requirement of your friends to store extra bags of blood, or is that part of Reed thinking he's a superhero?"

"The shirts." His chest shook with a laugh, followed by a groan as he clutched the wound in his shoulder. "Yeah, don't ask me why, but there's not a single shirt in his possession that doesn't have some kind of superhero logo on it. The guy's obsessed."

"That was clear while he was stitching you up. Kept telling me all about one of the movies he saw last week. I had no idea what he was talking about." She hadn't really had time to keep up on anything outside her own personal investigation into whoever'd stolen from the foundation's donations accounts other than a few baby books. "Guess I've been out of the loop for a while. I don't even know if you're living in the same apartment, or if you started seeing someone else after we…"

Air caught in her lungs. He'd kissed her back at the ranch. He wasn't the kind of man to kiss a woman while another waited for him to finish up his assignment, but that didn't mean he hadn't quickly moved on after her arrest. Didn't mean he hadn't replaced her.

"You're asking if I've been with anyone else since we split up?" he asked.

She shouldn't care. They weren't together anymore, and they didn't have plans to change that in the future. No matter what happened with the investigation, they'd agreed to be active in their daughter's life, but tension still flittered down her spine as she put a few more inches of space between them. Part of her did care—too much—and she wasn't sure what to do with that. She didn't like this feeling— this hope—he'd changed his mind about cutting her from his life after discovering the truth she'd been framed. Because anytime she'd given in to that sensation, she'd always been the one to get hurt, the one left behind. She moved to get out of the bed. "I'm sorry. It's not any of my business."

Calloused fingers wrapped around her arm, preventing her from escaping the warmth of the sheets, and she turned back into him. Beckett leveled his gaze on her, and everything inside her balanced on the edge of some invisible cliff waiting for his answer. One word. That was all it would take, and she'd fall. He released his hold on her arm and threaded his fingers through the hair at the base of her neck. "There hasn't been anyone but you, and when we were out there together, fighting to stay alive, I realized I didn't want there to be."

His admission cut through her, and her mouth dropped open. "What?"

"I made a mistake. After your arrest." Sliding his hand down her neck, along the most sensitive part of her throat, Beckett followed the trail of her collarbone. Fire erupted in the wake of his touch. In the past few months she'd known her body could feel pain, trauma, betrayal and numbness, usually more than one at a time, but she'd never felt this. This…connectedness to another human being. This craving. The muscles along his arm rippled as he ventured over her sternum and scorched a path toward her navel, resting where their baby thrived. "After we fled into the woods, you said I was so determined to make you the enemy, I refused to see if there was the tiniest shred of evidence proving your innocence. And you were right."

Her heart jerked in her chest. Deep down, she'd known that to be true, but there'd still been a piece that'd wanted her to be wrong. Hearing him admit it now… She didn't know what to say to that. Didn't know what he wanted her to say.

"I was so angry about what my father did to our family, I've been blinded from seeing anything other than the black and white in front of me. Good vs. bad. Guilty vs. innocent. People who hurt others vs. those who don't." He fisted his hand and dug it into the mattress between them. He cast his gaze down, refusing to meet her eyes. "Whenever I asked about your family, you dodged the question or would change the subject. I felt like you were keeping me at a distance the entire time we were together, hiding something, and after I got my hands on those sealed records, I was so positive I was seeing the real you for the first time. The criminal you didn't want me to know about. There were so many similarities between your case and my father's, I automatically equated all of that hatred and rage I had for what he'd done with you, but I was wrong. About everything, and I'm sorry. I know you had nothing to do with stealing those donations, and I'll spend the rest of my life trying to make up for my mistakes if that's what you need from me."

Tears burned in her eyes as the last of the barrier she'd built between them shattered.

"I'm sorry, too. Keeping my past from you had nothing to do with you and everything to do with me, Beckett. I never meant to keep you at arm's length. I just…wasn't ready to face it yet. All that pain, the consuming shame every time I thought about what'd happened with my brother." Raleigh framed his face with one hand, forcing him to look up at her. The dark, swirling blue depths of his eyes broadcast the internal war struggling to break through the surface. His beard tickled her palm as she stroked her thumb along his jaw. "But being with you these past couple of days, having to relive that part of me, confronting it openly and honestly, has finally forced me to get rid of this weight that's been suffocating me for years. You did that for me, and that counts for a lot more than you give yourself credit for."

"You give me too much. I told you I'd always be there for you. Then I disappeared when you needed me the most." He turned his mouth into her palm, anchoring her hand against his face with his, and kissed the sensitive skin below her fingers. "I was a coward, and you deserved a whole hell of a lot better than me."

"Good thing I'm the one who gets to decide what I deserve." Raleigh leaned into him, pressing her mouth to his softly. After everything they'd been through, how much he'd risked to keep her safe, coupled with his apology, the hurt she'd been holding on to for the past few months released a bit of its grip from her chest. Heat raced down her neck and across her shoulders as he rotated onto his back, dragging her with him, and a smile broke through her control. "I think you misunderstood. Right now, what I deserve looks like a US marshal making me breakfast."

"You got it." His laugh resonated through her, and she fought to memorize every second. There'd been times after her escape from federal custody she'd tried to remember that laugh, what it'd been like to wake up beside him, how it'd felt to have him warm her when a draft came through their apartment. In the end, they'd just been fragments of memory, but this… She'd never forget this. Beckett slid his legs over the side of the bed, then turned to press his hands into the mattress as he claimed her mouth in a dizzying kiss. The sweats he'd borrowed from Reed outlined thick lines of muscles in his legs and calves, and she couldn't help but enjoy the view. "Eggs, waffles and sausage coming right up. Don't go anywhere."

She'd been running for the past four months,

constantly looking over her shoulder, worried she wouldn't have the chance to clear her name before being taken back into custody. But here, she felt safe, protected, wanted. She wasn't going anywhere. "Wouldn't dream of it."

Chapter Ten

A baby.

He hadn't gotten the chance to fully consider what that meant. They'd spent the past two days running for their lives and trying not to get shot, but the news was starting to sink in now. Beckett shot his arm out to flip the eggs in the pan. Fried. Just the way she liked them. The timer of the waffle iron chirped, the entire kitchen a mess of waffle mix, eggshells, milk and cooking oil. Hell, their daughter wasn't even here yet, and the sinking sensation of doubt had already started creeping in. How were they supposed to do this? Clearing Raleigh's name of the embezzlement charges would take work, but the fact she'd escaped federal custody and gone on the run could make it so she'd have to serve some jail time. For how long, he didn't know. Guess it depended on the judge, but she'd broken the law, and while people changed—while he'd changed— the law didn't.

Right now, he couldn't fully tell the woman he'd

left in that bed was pregnant, her body almost as lean as he remembered. He didn't know a whole lot about babies, but that baby wouldn't wait around for her mother to pick a good time to make her debut. Beckett slid two eggs onto a plate and set the pan back on the stovetop. He hadn't asked to be a father, but he was going to be one anyway. He wasn't going to avoid his responsibility to that baby's creation. He had a steady job with the Marshals, an apartment. He could support their daughter while Raleigh got back on her feet. They'd have to work out a custody-and-visitation agreement after she was born, or…

His gaze settled on the stairs leading up to the single bedroom. Or maybe this thing between him and Raleigh could be more. Maybe he could have everything he'd ever wanted. Everything they'd both wanted for themselves but never got the chance. A family without secrets, without lies and resentment or loss. Just the three of them.

The smoke detector pealed from overhead, shocking Beckett back into reality. Within seconds, the rest of the detectors joined in from all over the cabin. His ears rang as he dashed to get the waffle burning in the iron free with a fork and his hands. Smoke dived deep into his lungs. Blistering heat burned his fingertips until he finally got the blackened mess free of the metal and into the kitchen sink. After unplugging the device, he flipped on the water and doused the charred remains of Raleigh's breakfast until the smoke cleared. He gripped the edge of the glossy black countertop. His throat burned. Yeah, he was definitely ready to be a dad. At least their daughter would be living off milk for those first few months. No need for her to have to suffer with his cooking skills. He tossed a kitchen towel across the room. "Damn it."

"That's not exactly what I had in mind when I asked for breakfast, but I appreciate the effort." The sound of bare feet padding down the stairs and across the hardwood flooring raised the hairs on the back of his neck, and suddenly he couldn't think. Couldn't breathe. Dark hair tousled from sleep, Raleigh was a vision unlike any he'd seen before. Long, lean, flawless in nothing but one of Reed's oversize superhero T-shirts, and his chest constricted. She smoothed her hands over the island countertop, the hints of green in the stone almost a perfect match for her eyes. "Need help? I've heard I make a mean glass of orange juice."

He couldn't hold back the laugh escaping his chest. Yeah, she did. "I was the one who said that after you started a fire in my apartment trying to soften the chocolate hazelnut spread in the microwave for your toast."

"Okay, so I accidentally put the jar in the fridge after sneaking some spoonfuls in the middle of the night." She lifted one shoulder in a shrug, angling her chin to the point she actually looked innocent as he wiped down the waffle iron. "I didn't think it would turn into a brick, and I was positive I'd gotten all the foil off the edges before I put it in the microwave."

"That wouldn't have held up in court if my landlord had moved forward with his lawsuit." Pouring the rest of the batter into the now decharred iron, he set the timer. "But now that you mention it, orange juice would be great."

"I'm on it." She moved around the counter, all grace and beauty as though the past couple of days hadn't affected her in the least or that they hadn't nearly died out there, and hell, he admired her for that. He'd spent the entire night envisioning how far he would've gone if Emily Cline had finished what she'd started, if he'd lost Raleigh and their baby. She ducked her head into the fridge, her shirt hugging her in all the right places, but Beckett could only zero in on the stain blossoming through the shirt from her side. "Any word from Reed or your office about the mess we left at the ranch? Can't imagine they're too happy—"

"You're bleeding again." He dropped the fork he'd been holding while waiting to pry the waffle free and closed the distance between them. The tang of metal on granite resonated in his ears as she closed the fridge, and she stared up at him. He threaded his hand between her arm and her rib cage to get a better look.

Arching the bottle of orange juice overhead, she studied the spread of red across her side. "Damn.

I have a feeling Reed isn't going to let me raid his closet anymore after he finds out about this."

"Sit down." He unplugged the waffle iron, took the bottle of orange juice from her and set it on the counter, then maneuvered her back until her knees hit the edge of one of the kitchen chairs. A combination of her natural scent and Reed's sank in his chest like a rock as she sat, and a dose of fire burned through him. He trusted the deputy, respected the hell out of him, but Beckett would break the bastard's nose if he came anywhere near what was his. Dropping to one knee, he suppressed the groan as the stitches in his thigh protested. His. What the hell was wrong with him? Two days ago he'd been fantasizing about handing her over to the feds, and now he was thinking of all the ways they could make a life for their daughter if given the chance. "I need you to…let me see the wound."

Which meant seeing anything going on under that shirt.

"Right. Not weird at all. Just exposing myself to a man who I used to sleep with so he can see what's wrong with my stitches. Not a big deal." The words carried a hint of sarcasm, that specific tone she'd use to neutralize any situation she didn't want to confront. She rolled her shirt higher, exposing long lines of pale, smooth skin and the pattern of moles he'd memorized that first night they'd been together. Tasteful beige underwear edged with lace skimmed the tops of her thighs, and suddenly he didn't dare touch her.

Not something so perfect, so beautiful. So deserving of better than anything he could offer.

But he'd try. Because he couldn't let the anger he'd held on to for all these years—the hatred for what his father had done—touch her or their baby. Neither of them deserved to feel that kind of pain or to feel the effects of his past trauma, and for the first time as he stared up at Raleigh, he realized he didn't either. Every decision Beckett had made over the past twenty years had led him to this moment, led him to becoming a US marshal. His father had led him here. He protected the innocent because he hadn't been able to protect his mother when he was sixteen. He hunted fugitives because he hadn't been able to find any kind of evidence of Hank Foster or the money he'd stolen after the son of a bitch had disappeared. He went out of the way for the men and women he worked with because he couldn't stand the thought of losing anyone else to the people he brought to justice. Everything he did, everything he said, was because of someone else's actions, and hell, that moment of losing the only family he'd had left had controlled him his entire life.

But it wasn't just him anymore. He was going to be a father to a baby girl, a coparent with Raleigh, and he couldn't let the past dictate his future. Not anymore. He wasn't sure he'd ever be able to forgive his father for what he'd done, but that single event didn't have to control him from here on out. Didn't have to hold him back from being happy. He had the power to choose, to let go, move on.

And he was choosing this.

Right here. Right now. Choosing Raleigh. Choosing their baby.

They were going to be a family.

"Beckett?" His name on her lips raised the temperature of the room by at least ten degrees. Or was it his heart rate that couldn't keep up with the rest of his body? Bloodied gauze lined with tape crinkled at the edges as she breathed. Raleigh tried to get a better look at the wound. "You look like you've seen a ghost. Is it worse than you thought?"

"No. I… You've done everything in your power to protect this baby, even against me, and I can't wait to see what kind of mom you'll be when she's born." He set his hand against her side, her body heat warming him straight down to his bones. His calluses caught on smooth skin as he peeled back the layer of gauze and tape. Thankfully, the stitches Reed had sewn in hadn't torn, but he'd need to clean out the area around the wound again and change her dressing. "I know I was another person in the long line of people who've hurt you, but if you'll let me, I'd like to be there for you both. Appointments, parenting classes, the birth. I can help with setting up the nursery or finding you an apartment when this is over, or if you want a custody agreement, I'll respect that, too. Whatever you're willing to let me have, I'll take it. I just don't want to screw this up. If you give me the chance, I want to be there for you and the baby, to prove I can keep my promises."

Her mouth parted. Her eyes went wide. "You want to do this together?"

"More than anything," he said.

"I don't…" Tension shot across his shoulders as mere seconds slipped past one after the other. Raleigh licked her lips, his attention homing in on the softness of her mouth before she nearly knocked him out cold with that gut-wrenching smile of hers. "I'd like that, but only on one condition. You have to change all of her dirty diapers."

Beckett laughed as he straightened on his knees and threaded his hand through the hair at the base of her neck. "You got a deal."

HE WANTED THEM to have another chance. To be a family.

Raleigh slipped from the bed, the hardwood floor cold under her bare feet as she reached for her discarded clothing a few feet away. They'd spent nearly the entire day talking, debating baby names, imagining what a combination of the two of them would look like, and she stretched all the stiff muscles she'd forgotten existed. Her stitches tugged at the fresh gauze he'd taped over her side, and she stopped short of straining the wound farther. It'd been a long time since she'd felt much of anything, but she felt this. Whatever this was between her and

Beckett. The tightness in her chest had lightened. It was easier to breathe. They'd been together for six months before the FBI had arrested her, but the connection they'd shared over the past few days somehow seemed different. Stronger. Changed.

What that meant for the future—if they had one as anything more than coparents—she didn't know, but after everything that'd happened, she was willing to find out. As much pain and hurt she and Beckett had caused one another, they'd agreed on one thing from the beginning: giving their daughter the life she deserved. Most of all she deserved two parents who would always be there for her, always love her, no matter what. Hypothetically, if those parents lived together in the same home, even loved each other, their baby could have a better shot at happiness.

Studying him from over her shoulder, she couldn't help but smile at the idea of waking up to this sight every morning, just as she'd imagined back at the ranch. The only thing missing was the crib that would be positioned nearby in a short few months. Everything else she needed was right in front of her. The smile weakened.

She'd envisioned it so many times after her arrest, but that deep-seated part of her still clung to the fear Beckett would be there for all the appointments and everything that came with preparing to give birth, not for her but for their daughter. Which, honestly, she should be grateful for. There were so many children orphaned by mothers who hadn't made it through the birthing process because the fathers weren't around to take responsibility. So many babies growing up in foster care as she and her brother had. She'd believed him when he'd promised to always be there for them. Because this was his baby, too. He was the kind of man to do whatever it took to ensure their daughter was loved, but he'd promised her the same thing before she'd been arrested. Now she was on the run.

Raleigh clung to her side as she stood, midafternoon sunlight gliding across her skin. Soon, they'd clear her name of the embezzlement charges. She'd have to appear in court for fleeing federal custody, even though she'd been wrongly accused in the first place, but afterward they'd get the chance to move on with their lives. A deeper part of her, one she hadn't dared investigate over these past three days, hoped that he'd meant together. Not as coparents, but as something more.

Her mouth watered as the craving for fresh fruit that'd woken her from her nap consumed her focus.

Padding down the stairs leading to the main floor, Raleigh ignored the colder temperatures on this level and headed for the fridge. Over the past few weeks her body temperature had been slowly climbing higher to the point she'd had to put the air conditioner in her aunt's cabin at risk of freezing up. Cool air cascaded across her exposed skin as she focused on the container of fresh grapes on one shelf. "Your dad makes a mean waffle, but we've got the good stuff now, baby girl."

An electronic ping registered from the small living room, which really only consisted of a modern-looking gray couch, a coffee table and barely any leg room. Popping the plastic grape container, Raleigh carried her snack toward the phone she'd taken from the shooter's vehicle on the coffee table. She wrapped her fingers around the thin frame. The screen lit up again as she raised the phone. It vibrated in her hand. An incoming call, but not from Beckett's contact list off his SIM card. The number wasn't stored in his contacts, but Raleigh knew that number. She'd dialed it over a hundred times over the years. "Calvin?"

She dropped the container of grapes. Both the local police department and the US Marshals had reports from the EMTs at the scene that he'd lost too much blood in his house for him to survive. Or was this whoever'd attacked him? Whoever'd framed her for stealing all that money? The phone stopped vibrating. A notification for one missed call slid across the screen. A different-pitched ping reached her ears as a new message arrived. She couldn't read it without entering Beckett's password. Raleigh glanced up the stairs, listened for any kind of movement before swiping her thumb across the screen. She had to know.

The screen bled from black to a white background with five words highlighted in a blue bubble.

"Pick up the phone, Raleigh." The thin metal frame vibrated again, startling her. Another incoming call from the same number. Her mouth dried. Hand shaking, she hit the green answer button on the screen and brought the phone to her ear. "Hello?"

"Raleigh, thank goodness you're okay." A graveled exhalation filtered through the phone as her former business partner's familiar voice nearly forced her to collapse in relief. "They haven't gotten to you yet."

"Calvin? I thought… They told me you were…" She turned toward the windows, looking out over the expanse of the trees and mountains. The cabin sat higher up the mountain, and she was afraid their connection wouldn't last long. He'd been declared missing less than two days after his wife, Julia, had called the authorities when she'd found the blood in their home, and the local police hadn't recovered a body. Calvin had to know the Marshals and the FBI were keeping up-to-date on his personal phone through phone records. They'd notice the call to this phone. They'd run the number and pinpoint where she was, who she was with. They couldn't waste time. "Tell me you're okay. All that blood at the scene—"

"I'm alive, but I barely made it out of my house. Your assistant, Emily, she was torturing me for information about another account, one the feds haven't linked to the investigation, but I didn't know anything. I only had what you'd shown me before the FBI showed up at the office." His unsteady breathing pierced through the slight ringing in her ears. He was out of breath. Possibly injured. "After I escaped, I ran. I got rid of my credit cards and tried to stay off the radar. I've been staying at a motel outside of Portland, but I think I might've been followed. What the hell is going on? Are you safe?"

"I'm safe." She'd done this. She'd brought him into this. Pressing one hand against the cool window, she forced herself to breathe through the heat climbing her neck. Cold worked down her arm and into the center of her chest. She'd ruined an innocent man's life trying to uncover the truth to save her own. "Calvin, this is all my fault. They came after you because I showed you the evidence I'd uncovered concerning the missing donations. They couldn't get to me while I was in federal custody, so they targeted you, and I'm so sorry. I'm going to fix it. I promise. I'm going to find the people who are doing this."

"Raleigh, listen to me. This isn't your fault. Just be sure to watch your back. Don't trust anyone. Understand? Especially the feds. Who knows how far this reaches?" Static preceded a loud thump on his side of the line. Calvin lowered his voice to a whisper. "I think they found me. Take care of yourself and remember what I said. Don't trust anyone."

The line died.

"Calvin?" Raleigh checked the screen. The timer

had frozen. He'd hung up on her, and fear slithered through her. She called the number back, but it went straight to voice mail. Her heart rate hiked into dangerous territory as she tried again.

Heavy footsteps echoed down the stairs, and she instantly deleted the record of her former business partner's call and message. Calvin had been targeted because of her, which meant someone had intel that she'd reached out to him in the first place. "Raleigh? I thought I heard you talking to someone. Everything okay?"

Don't trust anyone. Especially the feds. Calvin's warning played over and over in the back of her mind as she faced Beckett. She'd known and worked with Calvin Dailey for years. Not just within the foundation but personally. She had no reason not to trust him. They were still in danger, and if he was sure he was being followed back to wherever he'd been hiding, she had to keep her guard up, too. Because Calvin was right. They didn't know how far the corruption within the foundation extended, and she wasn't going to put his life—or his family's lives—any more at risk than she already had. Her gut clenched. Which meant, as much as she hated the idea, she couldn't tell the US marshal standing in front of her Calvin was still alive. At least, not until they found whoever was behind the threat to Calvin's and her lives. She tried to school her expression, the phone still in her hand, but even she could tell her smile was forced. "I'm fine."

"The grapes scattered across the entire floor say otherwise." Suspicion played across his expression, and her heart sank toward her stomach. He was one of the best marshals in the state. Reliable, cautious, supportive. The second she committed to keeping him in the dark, she'd destroy any kind of relationship they'd rebuilt, but Calvin's life had been put in danger because of her. It would be again if she exposed the fact her former business partner was still alive. She wouldn't be able to live with herself if something happened to him. Or Beckett.

"Funny story. The baby craves fresh fruit almost constantly, so I came downstairs to get a snack, and I couldn't find the remote for the TV, so I picked up your phone." Half-truths were the best kind of lies. More believable. She slid her hand over her stomach for reassurance she was doing the right thing. Instead, a hint of the numbness Beckett had helped dissolve closed in. "Turns out I'm not so great at the words game as I thought. I may have lost my temper and the game to someone named Watson."

She was taking a shot in the dark. That was the other deputy marshal on his team, wasn't it?

"I've been close to deleting that game a dozen times because of him. I swear the bastard has the entire English dictionary memorized." A smile pulled the lips she'd been kissing less than a few hours ago thin. He closed the space between them, sliding warm hands down her arms, and relief coursed through her. Beckett took the phone from her hand and set it back on the table before heading toward the fridge. "Come on. I'll make you a proper snack. Anything you and the baby want."

She eyed the phone as she followed him into the kitchen. "Sounds perfect."

Chapter Eleven

There had to be something in the FBI's reports they could use.

Beckett used the trackpad on Reed's laptop to scroll through the FBI's and Portland Police Bureau's investigation files. Interviews of anyone who had access to the donation funds, including Emily Cline, witness statements from the foundation's financial services division, bank account and routing numbers, evidence logs from the scene at Calvin Dailey's home and lists of documents taken off the foundation's servers—it was all here.

It all pointed to Raleigh as the primary suspect.

Whoever'd set this entire game in motion had covered their bases. The feds' case had practically been gift wrapped for them with a damn bow and a silver platter, but Beckett wouldn't let them win. Raleigh was innocent. The proof was in the bullet wound in his shoulder, the stab wound in his thigh and the piece of shrapnel in her side. Emily Cline had been hired by whoever'd taken that money to tie up loose ends. That'd included the mother of his child. It was a miracle they'd gotten out of there alive, but the nightmare wasn't over. Not until they uncovered who'd framed her for embezzling those funds. Until then he'd make damn sure they never got another shot at her.

The sun dipped behind the surrounding mountains and cast rays of pink and orange across the main level of the cabin. Beckett slid his attention to the sleeping woman on the couch, the circles under her eyes lighter than a few days ago. They'd spent most of the afternoon talking about the baby, what symptoms Raleigh had been feeling up to this point, checking her wound. She'd even let him put his hand over her stomach in hopes he'd feel a kick. Didn't work, but despite the resentment he'd wedged between them, he'd missed having someone this close, someone he could trust. Damn, if he were being honest with himself, he'd simply missed her. Her fight, her drive, her dedication to make any given moment more awkward between them. A short laugh burst from his chest, but quickly died as reality set in. Only problem with disappearing into the bubble they'd created together was it didn't stop the real world from going on, and it wouldn't solve this case.

But he would. For her, for their family and their future. Because no matter how many times he'd tried to convince himself otherwise, she'd gotten under his skin.

Beckett turned back to the laptop and started where this had all begun. The foundation's accounts. According to Raleigh, nearly twenty people had access to that money, and he'd dig into every single one of them until he got a hit. He paged through the statements collected at the beginning of the investigation, then checked the real-time balances of the accounts and leaned away from the computer.

"That can't be right." All of the affected accounts had been frozen the moment the FBI caught wind funds were missing. The entire foundation had been shut down from operating as long as the case was ongoing. So why was there a difference between the account statement logged four months ago and the current funds in the account? None of that money should've been accessible. He clicked through to the transfer history, noting the user ID below each amount moved from the account. Dozens of transfers leading up to Raleigh's arrest, all totaling one penny short of ten thousand dollars, the threshold unflagged by the federal government, but the last transfer—the largest of them all—had been made one day after Raleigh's arrest. Before the bank had frozen the accounts on the feds' order. Only she couldn't have made that transfer while she'd been in FBI custody. He grabbed his phone and used the calculator app, subtracting the difference between the original statements and the current balances. His low whistle pierced through the silence. One million dollars had gone missing the day after the accounts had been frozen, in addition to the original fifty-point-five million.

He could take this to the district attorney. He could show the transfers—all of them—hadn't been conducted by Raleigh but by someone else using her credentials, but it wasn't hard evidence. The DA would argue she had someone working on the inside, or that Beckett's judgment had been compromised. That she could've gotten access to a device without the feds knowing, or any number of valid variables. The sight of her on his phone as he'd come downstairs a few hours ago flashed across his memory, but he pushed that theory into the small black box at the back of his mind. She didn't have anyone on the inside. She wasn't transferring funds out of her own charity's accounts, and his judgment hadn't been compromised. He knew exactly who she was and what she was capable of. Beckett paged through the more recent statements. The money had to have gone somewhere, to another account the feds hadn't flagged. All he had to do was find the leak, and this would be over.

"You figured out there's more money missing." Movement pulled him from focus as Raleigh pushed upright in his peripheral vision, one hand on her side, but she refused to let her expression show how much pain she was in, and his gut tightened. Always out to impress, to prove she was the strongest.

"Have you suddenly developed the ability to read

my mind?" He pressed back into the bar-stool cushion and ran a hand through his hair as frustration took hold. Nobody could move that much money without tipping off the executives or the FBI, considering Raleigh's arrest had put the entire foundation under the microscope. There had to be a reason it hadn't been flagged. "Or is it some kind of sixth sense that comes with being pregnant?"

"Maybe it's Reed's shirt giving me extra abilities." Her laugh resonated through him as she slid one hand across his shoulders. The scrape of her nails across his skin raised the hairs on the back of his neck, eliciting remnants of the electricity they'd shared during that kiss back at the ranch. Raleigh studied the laptop's screen. "I saw the difference in the statements a few weeks after my arrest. IT was supposed to cut off my access, and for a while I think they had, but then I saw a single transfer notification sitting in my email when I logged in a few weeks ago. Someone had turned my access back on and had used it to make one more transfer after my arrest. And to make it look like I was the one who'd done it."

Clear green eyes connected with his as she leaned into him. Her voice hollowed, and it took everything in him not to give in to his explosive need for her bubbling to the surface. "When Emily had me tied to that chair in the barn, she confirmed my suspicion there'd been additional funds funneled out of the accounts into one the feds hadn't flagged yet, but at the time, the only thing I could focus on was you. I didn't know if you were alive, if you were dead, what the hell I'd gotten you into. I've already lost everyone I care about, Beckett. I didn't want to lose you, too. Not again."

"Hey, hey, listen to me." Beckett stood, pulling her in to his chest. Right where she belonged. A perfect fit against him. As though she'd been specifically made to fill the hole he'd been living with nearly his entire life. She hooked both arms under his, caging him between her elbows. Her vanilla scent tickled the back of his throat, and he breathed her in with every last ounce of spare room he had in his lungs, making her part of him. Forever. As he wrapped her in his arms, the world— his sense of justice, integrity, service, everything he thought he'd been standing for all these years— crashed down around him. Even at the threat of torture and pain from a malicious killer, his fugitive had put herself at risk. For him. Damn it all to hell, he loved her for it. Was in love with her. "You didn't get me into this, remember? I came after you. I made the choice to see this through until the end, and we're not done yet. We've survived this long. You, me and our baby. As long as we're together, that's all that matters."

Nodding, she splayed her hand over his heart, her hair catching on his beard under his chin. "Together."

"We're going to figure this out. We're going to

find whoever framed you. No matter what happens, I'm not giving up. I'm not going anywhere. I'm here for you and the baby." Beckett combed his hands through her long dark hair. "It'd take a tedious amount of patience and power to hide behind the hundreds of transfers it's taken to pull a heist like this off. Every step they've made is recommitting to building a case against you that would require months if not years of planning. Which executives have been at the foundation the longest aside from you?"

"Calvin and I started the foundation three years ago." Raleigh slid out of his arms, swiping at her face. "I guess the next executive would be one of our lower-level chief officers. She took over some of my duties about a year ago. Everyone else has been with the foundation for less time than that."

His instincts prickled. "How did you and Calvin meet?"

"At another charity event. I was trying to find investors on my own, and we happened to be seated at the same table. We got to talking. I told him my idea to provide expectant mothers with resources and education to help lower birthing mortality rates, and he wanted to help." She folded her hands into one another as she talked. "We worked together to raise the initial capital we needed to bring education and services to mothers here in Oregon, then spent the next few months writing pitches to local

businesses and corporations for donations before
we went national."

"You didn't run a background check on Calvin?"
he asked. "Didn't ask why he was so interested in
helping accelerate your work? Why he approached
you?"

"Approached me? I just told you we were seated
at the same table at another charity event. What do
you mean?" Mesmerizing green eyes narrowed on
his. She took a step back, taking the heat she'd gen-
erated deep below his skin with her. Color drained
from her face, and he reached out for her in case she
lost her balance. She shook her head. "You can't…
you can't possibly think Calvin had anything to do
with this. He was attacked because I brought him
into this. I went to him with the evidence I'd collected, and now he's missing."

She held on to her side, and a different theory
hit him in the gut. The blood. Reed had an entire freezer full of stored bags of blood in case of
emergency. For a former combat medic and a US
marshal, that wasn't entirely unusual, but what if
whoever'd framed Raleigh had had the same idea?

"You're right. He's missing, but I don't think you
had any part in that. The Portland Police Bureau
hasn't found a body. Just a lot of DNA evidence
that could've been easily planted with a few bags of
stored blood." Beckett gripped her arms, compelling her to look up at him. To at least face the idea
it was a possibility. "You didn't bring your busi-

ness partner into this at all. It was the other way around. Raleigh, I think Calvin Dailey stole that money, framed you for embezzlement and faked his death to get away with it. You've been a mark from the beginning."

IT WASN'T POSSIBLE. Calvin wouldn't…

A high-pitched ringing filled her ears as she pulled out of Beckett's reach. Three years of conversations, of dinner parties, of late-night pitch writing came into question in a matter of seconds. Her hands shook as she pushed one through her hair. Calvin had escaped a hired killer. Not faked his death. He couldn't have stolen all that money. Wouldn't have framed her. They were friends, partners in building something they could be proud of. Right? He wouldn't…he wouldn't do this to her.

Raleigh closed her eyes as a wave of dizziness washed over her. The timing of his disappearance, the fact he'd known how to reach her on Beckett's phone. The easy answer would be to put his face in that dark silhouette that'd been at the front of her mind since her arrest. The pieces fit better than she wanted to admit. Calvin could have planned this from the beginning. He could've been the one to frame her to take the fall. Because she was an easy mark. Just like Emily Cline had accused her of being.

"Talk to me." Beckett's grip on her arms held her up as the entire world she'd built threatened to shatter right in front of her. "Tell me what's going through your head."

"I…I need some air." She didn't know what else to say, what to think. She couldn't breathe without her chest tightening, and it felt as though the walls were closing in on her. She had to get out of here. Tugging out of Beckett's hold, she pushed past him toward the sliding back door of the cabin. She moved on autopilot, and within seconds, freezing air worked deep into her lungs. The outdoor scent of pine and earth—more pronounced than Beckett's natural aroma—filled the dark, empty spaces clawing for escape inside. Raleigh clutched on to the wood railing with everything she had. She'd barely processed the fact she was pregnant with Beckett's baby and had unshouldered the emotionally traumatic weight she'd carried her entire life, and now she was supposed to accept her closest confidant had turned her into a criminal? The muscles in her jaw ached as she clenched her back teeth. No. Anger blotted out the beauty and expanse of wilderness stretching miles in every direction as she dug her fingernails into the railing. If Calvin was responsible for her arrest—for everything—he hadn't just done this to her. He'd put her baby at risk, and she wasn't going to let him get away with it.

The sliding glass door protested on its track from behind. She didn't have to turn around to know he'd followed her. Her back warmed as Beckett drew near, and right then she wanted nothing more than to pretend he wasn't a US marshal and she wasn't his fugitive, but hiding from the truth didn't change anything. Hiding problems didn't heal them. She had to face it.

"He's alive. Calvin. He called me on your phone." Raleigh notched her chin over her shoulder, keeping him in her peripheral vision as he settled both elbows against the railing beside her. "That's who I was talking to right before you came downstairs. He convinced me Emily Cline had tortured him for information on the secondary account, like she'd threatened us, and I believed him. I agreed to keep his secret because I thought I was the one who'd put him in danger by coming to him with the evidence in the first place. I lied to you." Heat climbed her neck and into her face. She'd lied to a US marshal, but it was more than that. She'd lied to him, the one person who'd willingly positioned himself between a hired gunwoman and her and promised to protect their unborn baby, and she hated herself for it. She'd have to accept the consequences, whatever they may be, and her heart hurt thinking of all the possibilities of what that meant. Of losing him again.

Because over the past few days, she'd let herself care about him again. Cleaning her wounds from the bark, giving up the last of his food and water for her, taking on a professional killer so she could escape. He'd carefully chiseled his way through the hardened exterior she'd built from being unwanted for most of her life, and now there was nothing left.

Nothing but him. Whether he'd kept his word to see this investigation through to the end because of the pregnancy, his job with the Marshals or for her, it didn't matter. He'd made her feel wanted, desired even, and she'd hang on to this feeling as long as she could.

"You were right. I was just another mark, easily manipulated because building that foundation from the ground up made me feel valuable, like I was doing something good with my life for once. Calvin must've seen me for exactly what I was when we'd met. Desperate. Weak." Splintered wood bit into her palms. Emotion bubbled past her careful control. "I thought I was doing the right thing protecting Calvin, but that doesn't excuse the fact I lied to you. So I understand if you want to rethink our agreement concerning our daughter. We can work something out to where you won't have to see me after this is over—"

"Men like Calvin Dailey are master manipulators, Raleigh—that's their job. They enjoy hurting people and reaping the rewards of their hard work. No matter how many lives they destroy in the process." He was speaking from personal experience, and her stomach revolted. He'd lost his mother because of a con man. She could only imagine the thoughts running through his head right then. Hands intertwined, he stared out over the tops of the trees, gaze distant. Stars materialized overhead and added a bit of brightness to the blue of his eyes. He straightened, facing her before closing the small space between them. The length of his body pressed into hers, and she was forced to look up at him. He swiped her hair back from her face, and in an instant, warmth lightninged through her. "As long as I've known you, you've put everyone else's needs before your own. That's not weakness, Raleigh. That's courage, and it's one of the reasons I fell in love with you a long time ago. We're going to get through this, but only if we work together. We have to trust each other. No more secrets. No more lies."

Love? Her mouth parted, directing his attention straight to her lips, and an electrical zing lit up her insides. "You love me?"

"Out of all of that, that's what you choose to focus on during this conversation?" His smile pulled at something deep inside her as she lifted her arms behind his neck, careful of the wound in his shoulder. His hands dipped to her waist as though he needed her to anchor him right there on the back deck, and Raleigh was more than happy to let him take advantage. His smile disappeared as he settled those bright blue eyes on her. "You've been taking care of everyone else your whole life. It's time to put yourself first, Raleigh. Don't think about what you want for other people. What do you want? Right now, right here. Tell me what you want."

"I've only wanted one thing my whole life." Her mouth dried. She'd never admitted this to anyone, never admitted it to herself. Nobody had asked her what she'd wanted before, but her answer had always been there, waiting on the tip of her tongue from the very first foster home she could remember. It'd burned each time she'd reached out to someone, only to be used and discarded all over again, as Calvin was doing now. If there was one lesson she'd learned over the years of constant disregard, it'd been the people she'd cared about the most had always had the ability to do the most damage. Including Beckett. Raleigh trailed a path down his arms with her fingertips, memorizing every valley, every ridge in his build beneath the ridiculous shirt he'd borrowed from Reed's closet. "All I've ever wanted was to feel loved by someone as much as I loved them. To have that connection to another person, to be appreciated without any demands, expectations or manipulations. Not because I served a purpose at that moment in their life or because they have an obligation to me." A heaviness lifted from her chest, making it easier to breathe as she looked up at him. "Someone to love me…for being me."

Seconds ticked by, a full minute. Her heartbeat echoed at the base of her skull. She needed him to say something. Anything.

"There's only one thing I've ever wanted from you." Beckett raised his hand, rough calluses catching on the skin of her jaw as he scorched a path from her earlobe to her chin. Heated sensations battled the cool air slicing through the trees, but a shiver still racked her spine. Not from the temperatures. From him. Always from him. "That's for you to be happy. No conditions, expectations or demands. After everything you've been through in your life, you deserve a happily-ever-after. I don't care if you're pregnant with my baby or someone else's. You're not an obligation to me, and I want to be the one to give you everything. Every second of every day, I'll spend the rest of my life proving it to you, if that's what you need. Starting now."

He reached into his back pocket, pulled a piece of folded white paper free and handed it to her.

"What is this?" Confusion flooded through her. Dry corners slipped against her fingertips as she unfolded the single piece of paper and read the first few lines. Her heart threatened to beat straight out of her chest as understanding hit. "This is a letter of resignation from the US Marshals Service. Dated the day after my escape from federal custody."

Before he'd known she was pregnant.

"I was going to come after you one way or another, Raleigh Wilde," he said. "Because I'm not finished with you."

Tears burned in her eyes. Sincerity laced his words and anchored into the familiar sea of blackness she'd held on to inside for so long. From that single point something new chased back the loneliness, the isolation.

Raleigh lifted up onto her toes and brought his mouth level with hers. The slightest graze of his lips sent a rush of frantic sensation through her. His beard tickled the sensitive skin around her chin and cheeks, heightening her five senses to a whole new level. Carefully curated control—the kind she'd always needed to protect herself from becoming too attached to anyone around her—slipped through her fingers as he dug his hands into her lower back and maneuvered her back through the open sliding glass door. He loved her, and for the first time she could remember, freedom, unlike anything she'd experienced before, coursed along every nerve ending she owned, every muscle, every bone, until she felt like she might explode. "I believe you."

A moan escaped up his throat as Beckett directed her toward the counter, then hauled her onto the island, the cold of the granite more shocking to her central nervous system than she'd expected. The pain from both the bullet wound in his shoulder and the stab wound in his thigh must've spiked when he'd lifted her, but her marshal never let it show. Didn't so much as break their kiss. He was only focused on her, and a different kind of warmth penetrated through the layers she'd built over the years. "Back at the ranch, you told me this wasn't what you wanted. So I'm going to need you to be clear right now. What do you want from me?"

She loved him, too.

"You, Beckett." Her fingers ached as she fisted

his shirt and positioned him between her knees. Pressure released from beneath her rib cage as she breathed into his mouth. "All of you."

Chapter Twelve

Something had changed between them. Something significant he couldn't explain, but the resulting awareness he'd experienced after Raleigh had admitted her deepest desire to be valued above all else didn't press him to dig deeper. She'd trusted him, where so many others had let her down before, and he'd do whatever it took to deserve that trust.

Of all the stories his daughter would hear about her mother when she was old enough, they wouldn't be about fear or loss or manipulation. No. She'd know how strongly, bravely and fearlessly Raleigh fought for her when the world threatened to bring her down. This baby would grow up knowing how to rely on herself through every battle, every struggle that pushed back at her, because of the example of the woman asleep beside him, and Beckett couldn't wait to see it for himself.

Raleigh hadn't felt important to anyone her entire life, but she was everything to him.

And he wasn't about to lose her again.

He slowly drew his legs over the edge of the bed, soreness rocketing through him. There had to be something he was missing in those files, something not even the FBI had caught.

"If you think you're getting out of this bed, Marshal, think again." A smile pulled at her kiss-burned lips as she lay facedown beside him. She shifted beneath the sheets, hypnotic green eyes settling on him as she rolled onto her side. Raleigh wedged one arm under her head, all that gorgeous hair stark against the white pillowcase, and wiggled her eyebrows higher in a feigned attempt at seducing him. "I'll share some of the chocolate I found under the mattress if you reconsider."

A laugh reverberated through him. Damn, he loved her. The mattress dipped under his knee as Beckett planted a kiss on her forehead, afraid anything more would, in fact, stop him from getting out of the bed. He straightened. Collecting another set of clothes from Reed's clothing rack, he shoved his feet into a pair of jeans slightly tighter in the waist than he was used to. "As much as I'd love to break into Reed's weird, secret collection of mattress food, Calvin Dailey is still a suspect we need to look into. Until we're certain he's the one behind those missing funds, you're in danger, and if you want me to be able to pay child support for our daughter, I've got a job to do."

Raleigh sat up on the bed, the sheet clasped against her chest, and he couldn't look away. Temptation to do exactly as she asked flared as he forced himself to reach for a clean T-shirt from the rack. "That's the first time you've said *our* daughter."

"You're right." He slumped onto the bed beside her, his hand automatically reaching for the slightly firm section of her stomach where their baby grew. Beckett kissed her bare shoulder. "Guess it finally feels like we're on the same team."

"Always." She lifted his chin with one finger and slipped her mouth over his, and he was lost in her all over again.

"That's cheating." His laugh filled the room a second time, and it took every last ounce of strength and determination he had left to pull away. "I'm going to check out the transcripts from Calvin's interview conducted by the feds. Feel free to join me after you're dressed."

"Fine, but I'm keeping all of the mattress chocolate for myself," she said.

He made his way down the stairs. On the main level, he righted the laptop he'd pushed across the kitchen island to get to Raleigh and brought it out of sleep mode. Hell, his shoulder and thigh still hurt after that one, but at the time, the pain hadn't bothered him at all. He'd just wanted her. His blood heated at the memories of his name on her lips, the feel of her surrounding him, the echo of exhalations as they'd climbed into ecstasy together. But as long as the threat was still out there, neither Raleigh nor their baby would be safe, and he'd never live with himself if something happened to her on his watch. Not when they could give each other everything they'd ever wanted. Needed.

Beckett clicked through the FBI's case file straight to the interviews and statements. Calvin Dailey had been interviewed by an agent shortly after Raleigh's arrest, but nothing in the transcript gave them a leg to stand on that he was their man. What'd he expect? A full confession? The son of a bitch had claimed he hadn't known anything about Raleigh dipping into the foundation's funds, despite her official statement she'd handed over the evidence she'd collected straight to him two weeks before an anonymous tip pinned her as the FBI's primary suspect. But according to Calvin's statement, it'd sure broken his heart when he'd found out. Yeah, right. Beckett shook his head. Guys like Calvin Dailey were all the same, but Beckett had experience with his kind, and he sure as hell wasn't going to let another con man destroy his future. "Let's see if that's even your real name."

Logging in to the Warrant Information Network— WIN—used by marshals all over the country to conduct investigations, run warrant searches, handle threat management and keep an eye on witnesses in WITSEC, he typed the suspect's name into the search bar and hit Enter.

And froze as the man's photo stared straight back at him.

His knees threatened to drop right out from under him as nausea worked up his throat. He gripped the edge of the counter. The suspect was older, slightly worn around the edges, but Beckett would recognize that face anywhere. His instinct to check into the foundation's CEO had been right. Calvin Dailey wasn't the man's real name. Hell, Beckett wasn't even sure he'd ever known his real name, but he knew at least one other alias for the feds to trace.

"Reed seriously needs to consider the kind of chocolate that's worth stashing." Light footsteps padded down the stairs at his back as the muscles down his spine hardened. "Good chocolate is not supposed to have a diet aftertaste. I don't care how much he paid for it. None of that was worth saving."

His hands shook as the rage he'd tried to contain these past few days exploded through him. Adrenaline surged into his veins, the pain in both wounds pushed to the back of his mind. Everything about this case had felt too close, too familiar. He'd ignored those initial suspicions, attributed his feelings to the situation between him and Raleigh, but he'd been wrong from the start. "You knew, didn't you?"

"About the chocolate?" She crossed into his peripheral vision as she wrenched the refrigerator door open and reached inside for a bottled water. "I wish. Now I can't get that taste out of my mouth. Brushing my teeth didn't help."

"You were helping him this entire time, and I was too blinded to see it." The main level of the cabin blurred as Beckett turned on her, and those bright green eyes widened. The past year came into excruciating focus. The mugging, their whirlwind romance, her arrest, the pregnancy. Hell, even him finding out Calvin Dailey was still alive had probably gone off without a hitch. Every step had been meticulously timed and executed. Because if there was one thing he knew about that man in the photo, Calvin Dailey—whoever the SOB would become next time around—never did anything halfway. When he set out to destroy lives, he succeeded. Only Calvin Dailey wouldn't have been able to do it alone. "I've been racking my brain, wondering how on earth someone in the foundation was able to steal that much money without anyone else noticing but you. Now I know. You're working with him."

Venom dripped from his words as Beckett closed the distance between them. The tendons in his fingers ached as he curled them into fists. Had any of it been real, or had he just taken the bait?

"What are you talking about?" Color drained from her face, but she couldn't fool him. Couldn't pretend. Not anymore. What'd looked like vulnerability was a carefully constructed emotional response catered to him, to his reactions. Like the good con woman she was supposed to be, and everything he'd felt for her, every promise out of his mouth, ground into dust inside him. Raleigh tried to counter his approach until her back hit the refrigerator. There was nowhere for her to go this time. Nowhere for her to run. Not from him. "Beckett."

"You've been working with him this entire time, haven't you? Using me," he said.

The muscles along her throat flexed as she swallowed, the water bottle still clenched between her hands. "You're accusing me of partnering with Calvin Dailey to steal from my own foundation. Based on what evidence?"

"Come on. We both know that's not his real name." He struggled to control the fire burning through him as he reached for the cuffs he'd left on the counter beside the keys to the SUV. Cool metal pressed against his palm. "You might as well call him Hank Foster when you're talking to me."

"Calvin Dailey is…your father?" Disbelief coated her words. She stared up at him, her mouth parted slightly as though she were surprised by the information. Hank had certainly taught her well. Her exhalation reached his ears. She shook her head. "Beckett, I swear to you I had no idea—"

"Stop lying!" He slammed his free hand against the fridge above her head, his control razor thin. He'd survived the past twenty years living off his anger—his hatred—for that man, but with her he'd nearly forgotten that feeling. Now the familiarity of that rage wrapped around him. Supported him. Protected him from being that sixteen-year-old kid holding his mother on the floor as she died in his arms. He backed off and collected his shoulder holster loaded with one of Reed's backup weapons from the counter, threading his arms through the supports. "I'm guessing you didn't expect to be arrested four months ago. Your partner threw you under the bus because that's the kind of bastard he is, and as a backup plan you thought you could use me as a get-out-of-jail-free card. You'd appeal to my sense of justice, seduce me, and later down the road, you'd disappear." Beckett turned to her, lasering her with his glare. "Just tell me one thing. Was the pregnancy his idea or yours?"

Her expression smoothed, any hint of the vulnerable, soft woman she'd been slipping away by the second. In her place, the self-assured, driven fugitive he'd always known existed surfaced. "You didn't answer my question. You're accusing me of partnering with a con man to steal from my foundation. What evidence have you found to support that theory?"

"I don't need evidence. You're already a fugitive." Beckett let his hands slip from the refrigerator and pushed away. Grabbing her right arm, he spun her around and secured one cuff around her wrist. Then the other. "Raleigh Wilde, you are under arrest."

THE CUFFS CLICKED loud in her ears, and the invisible black hole he'd helped repair over the past few days engulfed her from the inside. Raleigh bit back the scream working up her throat as her heart shattered into a million unrecognizable pieces, worse than before, but she wouldn't cry. She wouldn't show weakness. Not in front of him. She'd trusted him, believed he'd keep his promises this time, and from the hardness in his expression, there was nothing she could say to make him see the truth. But that didn't stop her from trying. "You're making a mistake, Beckett. I didn't know Calvin was your father. I swear—"

"I'm not interested in anything you have to say. Now walk." His voice lacked the slightest hint of the emotions he'd shown her while they'd been here, and the empty space inside only spread faster. He'd said he'd fallen in love with her, that he'd be there for her and the baby. Had it all been a lie? Beckett gripped the cuffs between her wrists and maneuvered her toward the cabin's front door. "I risked my career for you, put my life on the line for you, and this is what I get for trusting a fugitive. The second I hand you off to the FBI, I'm going after Hank, and I'll never have to deal with you again. My lawyer will be in touch to make arrangements for custody after the baby is born."

He was going to take her baby from her.

"No." Raleigh wrenched out of his hold, twisting around to face him, and he automatically reached for the weapon he'd borrowed from Reed's arsenal upstairs. Her gaze lowered to his hand, then rose back to those defensive blue eyes. Would he shoot her? Would he risk his daughter's life out of his misdirected hatred for the man who'd threatened to destroy them? "I didn't have anything to do with

Calvin—" she closed her eyes as disbelief reared its ugly head and forced herself to breathe evenly "—Hank stealing that money. If after everything we've been through together, you still don't believe me, I can handle that. But you don't get to pretend what we had didn't mean anything to you and drive off into the sunset without facing me."

The veins along his forearms seemed to strain to break through the thin skin there, his hand still positioned over the gun in his holster. "What you can or can't handle no longer concerns me."

"Tell me you don't believe me." She battled to keep her face expressionless. She wouldn't back down until he said the words, until he confirmed her deepest, darkest fear. She wouldn't let him see how much his betrayal hurt, how he'd broken her down to nothing all over again. She wasn't going to let him see the destruction he'd caused. Not just for her but for their daughter. Raleigh stepped into him. "Lie to my face. Tell me you don't love me so we can both move on with our lives after you realize what you've done."

One second. Two.

"How could I love someone like you?" His words came through gritted teeth. "I don't even know you, and neither will our daughter."

The effect hit her as though she'd been impaled with a piece of shrapnel all over again. Her throat burned with the sob building at the edges. She'd forgotten how to breathe, how to move, and all she could do was nod as numbness spread through her. No thoughts. No sensations. Just a sea of comforting black she'd been retreating into her whole life. "Then let's get this over with."

Beckett reached over her shoulder and disabled the alarm panel before spinning her toward the door. Cold air worked under the superhero T-shirt and pale gray sweats she'd borrowed from Reed's clothing rack as he led her outside. Her bare feet caught on the splinters sticking out from the aged front porch of the cabin, but she kept moving at his insistence. Dark stains spotted the stairs as they descended, a bloody trail of breadcrumbs leading them to the SUV she'd used to get them to safety. When she'd believed he could finally move past the hatred that'd been tearing him apart since he was sixteen years old.

She'd been wrong.

Raleigh focused on the SUV as they approached. She could run. She could head straight for the trees and never look back, but she'd spend the rest of her life looking over her shoulder if she ran. Because Beckett Foster would never stop searching for her or for his daughter. The best chance she had of giving their baby the life she deserved—a family—would be to prove her innocence and fight for custody. No matter how long it took. No matter how much it hurt.

"What did Hank promise you if you helped him steal all that money? A cut of his share? That he'd leave the entire foundation in your hands and let you live out the rest of your life in peace?" His humorless laugh broke through the slight ringing in her ears. He wrenched the back passenger-side door open but held her arm to keep her from getting in. The keys jingled in his hand as he unlocked one cuff and hauled her hands above her head before securing her to the handle above the seat. Beckett stepped aside as she got in, his hand resting on the outer edge of the door. "I think him hiring Emily Cline to take you out tells you exactly what kind of man you've gotten involved with. Because of you our baby—my baby—is in danger, and if anything happens to her, it's on you. I hope you can live with that."

Nothing she said, no amount of evidence she presented to the contrary, would alter his belief about her or satisfy his anger. She doubted hearing it from the source of all that hatred would do any good either. Beckett had spent his entire life fighting to counterbalance the evil his father had carried out. She only hoped he understood it'd be a lifelong battle. Not with Hank Foster but with himself. She stared at the back of the front headrest as best she could with both hands secured over her head. "If it's all the same to you, I'd rather not talk the rest of the trip back to Portland."

"You got it." He slammed the door, the force quaking through her as she followed his movements through the windshield. Not yet. She couldn't break apart yet, but every step he took around the front of the SUV sealed her fate. He'd take her back to Portland. He'd hand her over to the FBI, and she'd never see him or her daughter again. Of all the promises he'd made over the past few days, this would be one he'd never break.

Tears burned in her eyes, and she ducked her chin to her chest as he pulled himself into the driver's seat. He didn't love her, but she'd been through this before and survived. With every foster family who hadn't been able to handle her violent attempts to protect her brother, with being forced to live with an aunt who'd only used them for an extra paycheck, with the loss of friends after her arrest. Then why, after so many others had discarded her out of self-ishness, did Beckett's admission hurt this much? He'd distanced himself from anything that had to do with her after her arrest four months ago, just as he was doing now. Why was this time any different?

Staring out the window, she couldn't focus on anything other than her opaque reflection in the glass. The answer was there, drowning in the storm of feelings reminding her she'd always be unwanted, worthless, unloved by everyone around her. That storm had built her into the woman who'd do whatever it took to succeed emotionally, professionally and physically, but this time…this time she'd let him in. She'd let her guard crumble for the off chance of building a life for their daughter, one where their baby would never doubt she was loved. But now

Raleigh would have to be the one to suffer the consequences.

The SUV's engine vibrated to life, and Beckett directed them down the single dirt access road leading down the mountain. The cuffs hit against the handle above her head as the vehicle climbed over wayward rocks and dips in the road. His gaze lifted to the rearview mirror, connecting with hers for the briefest of moments, and her gut clenched. The trip back to Portland would take at least two hours. She could do this. For hers and Beckett's daughter. *You never know how strong you are until being strong is the only choice you have.* Her brother's words echoed as a memory of him reaching down to help her to her feet after a particularly nasty fight with another foster brother landed her with two broken fingers and a bloody nose. She didn't have a choice now, but she'd sure as hell make sure her daughter did.

She caught movement through the windshield a split second before a bullet penetrated through the glass. Beckett's pain-filled groan filled the silence, and Raleigh ducked low as best she could in her seat as he veered the vehicle off the road. Her heart throbbed at the base of her skull. "Beckett!"

"Damn it. I'm fine." Cold air rushed through the hole in the glass as Beckett reached for his gun. He clutched his side. Blood spilled between his fingers, and before he could unholster his weapon, he slumped in his seat. Unconscious.

"Beckett?" Raleigh leaned forward as much as she could to reach him, but the cuffs kept her secured. She couldn't get to him. The road forced the SUV to course correct, and they were once again headed down the mountain, increasing speed as they approached a sharp turn ahead. She pulled at her restraints, a desperate growl slipping past her control. The pines up ahead were growing larger through the windshield. They were going too fast. They were going to crash.

Sitting back in her seat, she braced for impact as best she could. The vehicle's tires caught on the edge of the opposite side of the dirt road, and the vehicle flipped. The ground rushed up to meet her window. A scream tore past her lips as rocks shattered through the glass and scraped along her shoulder, but before she could take another breath, the SUV rolled again. The tree line and the ground blurred as her stomach shot into her throat. Then everything was still. Absolutely still.

A low thump reached past the haze closing in. Her body felt as though she'd been burned as cold air met the fresh layer of raw skin under the cuffs and the gravel embedded in her shoulder. She clutched the handle Beckett had cuffed her to and tried to sit up, broken glass and debris shifting under her heels, but the SUV had landed upside down in the middle of the road. There was no up. A deep groan reached past the echo of her uneven breathing, and her heart jerked. "Beckett."

The series of thumps grew louder. Closer. Footsteps? Hinges protested loud in her ears as her passenger-side door ripped open, and she closed her eyes to block the piercing sunlight as a dark outline closed in.

"Hello, Raleigh," a familiar voice said. Cold metal slipped between her skin and the cuffs before the steel links snapped. Her arms relaxed onto her chest as a second, more muscular outline reached in and pulled her from the vehicle. "You and I have some unfinished business to discuss."

Chapter Thirteen

"So this is what dying feels like." Beckett gripped the ambulance bay door as the EMT threaded another stitch into his side. His pain receptors screamed in protest, but lucky for him, the bullet had been a through-and-through. A few more stitches and a clean dressing and he'd be back out there hunting his fugitive.

"Stop getting shot, and you wouldn't have to go through this again." Chief Deputy Remington Barton adjusted the AR-15 strapped over her shoulder, barrel pointed down. A black long-sleeved T-shirt peeked out from under her dark tactical vest with US Marshals spread across the back. The radio specifically designed to reach the rest of the deputies on their team had been strapped to one side of the Kevlar, grazing her short black hair, but it was those intense blue eyes that said she was ready for the coming fight. Prepared to protect her team and get the job done. "Want to tell me I'm wrong about how close you are to this investigation again?"

He wasn't going to dignify that question with a response. Helicopter blades thumped loud from overhead. Last he'd checked, the dogs had tracked Raleigh's trail north, but they'd lost her scent as soon as she and whoever'd gotten her out of the SUV had crossed the river about two hundred feet into the woods. They had the entire Oregon US Marshals Service working this manhunt, but Raleigh was smart. She'd managed to escape federal custody once. He should've expected her to try again. "Any sign of her?"

"The footprints we tracked disappear at the river. Looks like whoever'd shot you and pulled her from the SUV carried her out, but we managed to pick up tire tracks on the other side until they meet up with the main road." Remi studied the scene as the sun arced over the western half of the sky. "Whoever was behind the wheel most likely headed west, but enough time passed between the accident and when we arrived on scene, they could be anywhere right now. We're running matches to narrow down the make and model of the vehicle from the tires and putting checkpoints in place. We'll catch her."

"She won't go back to her aunt's cabin. Too risky." Damn it. There was a piece of this case he wasn't seeing, something his gut had been trying to tell him from the start. He just couldn't think straight enough to figure it out. "What about Calvin Dailey? Any luck tracing the call he made to my cell?"

No. Not Calvin Dailey. Hank Foster. His bastard of a father was still hurting anyone he came into contact with, consequences be damned, only this time Beckett would be ready for him. He'd do whatever he had to, to make sure the SOB didn't hurt Raleigh. For his daughter's sake. Pressure built behind his chest as he studied the wreckage. He'd cuffed her to the handle above the back seat. She wouldn't have had any way to fight off the shooter if she was, in fact, innocent, as she'd claimed. The new set of stitches in his side stung, keeping him in the moment. There was no point imagining what'd happened after the crash. Raleigh wasn't innocent.

"The call was rerouted using an internet service. No location, but we've got units at the foundation and his home, and his photo and a list of possible aliases sent to every law-enforcement agent and officer in the state." Remi's ocean-blue gaze locked on him as Beckett shoved to his feet, her mouth lifting at one corner. "I'm sorry. Are you wearing one of Reed's superhero T-shirts?"

He stared her down. "They were the only clean clothes he had on hand."

"If you say so." The chief deputy surveyed the other marshals around them, her expression weary as she stepped into him and lowered her voice. The side of her weapon caught on his shirt. After reaching into her pants pocket, she handed him a thin piece of paper. "There was something else we found while we were following Wilde's trail to the river.

Something I have a feeling you wouldn't want anyone else to know about."

Beckett smoothed the thin paper, and a crushing weight took hold of his insides.

The ultrasound.

"You two were together twenty weeks ago," Remi said. "The baby's yours. That's why you wanted to help her clear her name."

Panic cemented his feet in place. His blood pressure spiked as he ran one hand through his hair. Raleigh had done everything she could to hang on to the evidence of her pregnancy these past three days. Hell, she'd slept with the ultrasound right next to the damn bed and kept it in her sweats pocket when she was up walking around the cabin. He ran his fingers over the fresh fold marks. No exceptions. She never would've left this behind.

Not unless she'd been unconscious.

Or taken against her will.

Which could mean… Raleigh was in danger. "Where did you find this?"

"Northwest. About fifty feet past the tree line." Authoritative blue eyes steadied on him, but Beckett was already maneuvering around his superior. "Beckett, she's a fugitive. You knew that when you took on this assignment, and I can't protect you if—"

"I don't need your protection. I'm going to save my family. With or without your help." The scene vanished to the back of his mind as he headed for the nearest SUV. Raleigh was out there. She was in the hands of a killer who'd used her to play out his sick game, and Beckett had accused her of being one of the masterminds. Damn it, how could he have been so stupid? He'd let his hatred for Hank Foster destroy the last remaining chance he had of moving on with his life, of having everything he'd ever wanted, because he couldn't let go of the past. If his father so much as broke a hair on her head, he'd kill the man himself.

His boots sank in the damp earth as Beckett wrenched open the door to Remi's SUV and climbed inside. Within seconds, he'd flipped the vehicle around and accelerated down the mountain. Pines thinned at the bottom of the road, his hands aching from his grip on the steering wheel. "I'm coming. I'm going to find you."

He had to think. Hank had spent the past three to four years as Calvin Dailey, but the man would still have his own habits, locations he would've visited over and over aside from the foundation or his home. Things the con man had been doing for so long, no alias could change. Beckett slowed at the bottom of the hill and shoved the vehicle into Park. He shouldered out of the SUV and rounded the hood. Dips in the old dirt road tried to trip him up, but that didn't stop him from crouching beside the fresh set of tire tracks. Remi had mentioned the driver of the vehicle had most likely turned west to head back to Portland, but this set of muddied tracks leading off the dirt road said otherwise.

East. Toward Mount Vernon.

Beckett straightened, gaze following the length of single-lane asphalt road about a mile off. The bastard was taking her back to where this had all begun twenty years ago. "He's headed to the ranch."

New stitches stretched across his wound tight as he hauled himself back into the driver's seat. Adrenaline brought everything into focus as he dropped the magazine out of the sidearm he'd borrowed from Reed's home arsenal and counted the rounds. There were no guarantees Hank had been working alone when he'd taken Raleigh. He'd hired Emily Cline to do his dirty work, but Beckett wouldn't be caught off guard this time. Not when his entire future was at risk.

He put the SUV in Drive and turned east on 26.

An undeniable rift tore through him at the thought of losing that future, at the thought of what he'd accused Raleigh of doing, at the thought of having to go back to the place where he'd lost everything that'd mattered to him as a kid. He'd spent most of his life trying to recover from the single event of losing his mother to violence, of having a father who'd chosen to hurt people. He'd put himself through high school, gotten his criminal justice degree, worked the ranch with his own two hands and gotten away from it all, but somewhere in the process he'd convinced himself he didn't need anyone.

There'd been one person in this world he could rely on when times got tough: himself. But deep down, somewhere he hadn't dared look in a long time, he knew he couldn't spend the rest of this life angry. On edge. Alone. Not when there was a woman out there who'd helped him forget all of that over these past few days, who'd…freed him from the control Hank Foster had held over him since he'd been sixteen years old.

Hell, he needed that weight gone. Needed her.

Raleigh had given him a reason to let the past die. She'd given him something to look forward to after all these years. One look from her—one touch—and the chaos he'd warred with for twenty years calmed, and he couldn't give up on that. Because she hadn't given up on him. Now it was his chance to return the favor.

Beckett reached for his phone, the screen brightening as he raised it, and sent the ranch's coordinates to the rest of the team. He pressed his boot flat against the accelerator to push the vehicle faster. The ultrasound he'd tossed into the passenger seat sat stark in his peripheral vision against the muted background. He reached for it, switching his attention between the dark photo of his and Raleigh's growing baby and the road ahead.

He'd known the day he'd have to face Hank was coming, and if there'd ever been a reason better than to settle the past, it was to save the two people who held his future. "I'm coming, Raleigh. For both of you."

EVENING LIGHT SLANTED at her feet through the old slats nailed over the only window in the room.

Raleigh rolled her head to one side. The out-of-date wainscoting at her back dug into her spine, her hands restrained overhead to some kind of exposed metal plumbing. Dust danced in the rays of sun, making it hard to decipher between the white spots still clinging to her vision and spores. Chunks of drywall littered the peeling linoleum flooring near the legs of an old kitchen set with a single chair. A vanity dresser took up most of the opposite wall, an odd choice considering this room had obviously once been a kitchen, but the framed photos lining the bottom of the mirror told of a family-centered space.

She closed her eyes as pain splintered through one side of her head. She and Beckett had been in an accident, which accounted for gravel embedded in the first few layers of skin of her shoulder. Beckett. He'd been shot, and… She couldn't remember anything after that. Light green flowered wallpaper curled along her side as Raleigh pulled at the rope to sit up.

"I always loved this wallpaper," someone said from beside her.

She jerked as far away from that voice as she could, but the ropes didn't have much give. Her heart shot into her throat as she realized how close he'd gotten. "Calvin. What…what are you—"

"Took us three months to agree on this paper."

His navy blue suit jacket and slacks accentuated dirt and dust streaking along his tall frame. Dark brown shoes knocked against hers as she leveraged her heels into the aging floor. Calvin's arms framed either side of his head, blocking her view of his face, but she'd know that voice anywhere. She'd trusted that voice for three years, never knowing what kind of man he really was, how far he'd go to hurt the people who cared about him the most. Not just her but Beckett, the families he'd conned twenty years ago, the women who wouldn't get the help they needed from the foundation they'd started together. Gray stubble peppered what she could see of his jaw, the wrinkles at the edges of his mouth somehow more pronounced.

He twisted his entire upper body to face her, steel-blue eyes putting her directly in his crosshairs, and her gaze lifted to the rope wrapped strategically around his wrists. Just like she'd been restrained. "My first wife and me. She would've liked you, you know. I knew the moment I met you at that charity function all those years ago, she would've liked you. In some ways you remind me of her. Headstrong. Stubborn. Guess she had to be, considering she'd been married to a man like me."

"You mean the kind of man who steals money from innocent, hardworking families and people in need?" Raleigh couldn't keep the bitterness out of her tone, even with them both tied to the same damn line of plumbing. He obviously hadn't been the one to cause the crash when the shooter had put a bullet in his son, but that didn't make Calvin—Hank— innocent either. "I know who you are, Hank Foster. I know what you've done and the people you've hurt."

His chin dipped toward his chest, that all-too-familiar voice tainted with something she couldn't quite put her finger on. "Beckett."

"He told me everything. You target innocent victims, prey on marks you can manipulate into doing what you want, consequences be damned." Years of trust, of friendship, slipped away as she faced him, and Calvin suddenly looked far older than she remembered. He might not be the current threat, but that didn't make him any less dangerous. He'd stolen victims' life savings, retirements, everything they'd had, and disappeared as though it'd never happened. "Was that what I was for you? Another mark in the long line of easy targets? Is that why you approached me at that charity event? You saw something you could take advantage of and turn a profit, no matter how many people got hurt in the process."

"You were never a mark, Raleigh, and I never profited from our foundation. Not a single penny. All my salary checks for the past three years? I donated them right back into the foundation we built together. I didn't want any of it." Hank Foster set the crown of his head back against the wall, staring up at the dilapidated ceiling threatening to crash down on them at any moment. He closed his eyes. "I stole that money twenty years ago. I did, and it destroyed my family. It got my wife—Beckett's mother—killed, left my son orphaned, and I've never been able to forgive myself since. The day I heard about what'd happened to her, that Beckett had been there to witness the entire thing, I gave it all back to the people I'd stolen from. Every dime." He locked trusting blue eyes on her. "When I met you, when you reminded me so much of my late wife, I realized starting this foundation with you would be a step in the right direction to fixing what I'd done. It might never be able to make up for all those people I hurt—especially my son—but I'll spend the rest of my life trying."

Truth resonated in his voice, and an acrid taste filled her mouth. Her stomach knotted. Everything that'd happened since the moment she'd been arrested had been carefully planned, calculated, but the tired-looking man restrained next to her didn't fit that description. Emotions she'd shut down after Beckett had arrested her and accused her of partnering with the thief surged to the surface. Relief, fear, guilt and curiosity tumbled over one another, and she didn't know which to process first. Her throat seized. "You…didn't steal the money, did you?"

"No." Footsteps echoed off the walls of an adjacent room, and Calvin turned toward the sound. "But I know who did."

A familiar outline centered in the doorway across the room, and a rush of memories materialized. The comfortable—almost caring—voice Raleigh hadn't been able to place after the crash, the oversize bolt cutters that'd snapped the links of her cuffs, the surprising strength it'd taken to pull her from the wreckage. Her attacker's long, lean frame shifted beneath a denim jumpsuit, shiny brass buttons and jewelry reflecting the dim light. Caramel highlights stood out from the waves of long blond hair fluttering around the woman's shoulders, and there, that beautiful, straight smile that'd welcomed Raleigh into her home so many times over the years flashed wide.

"Julia," she said.

Julia Dailey, Calvin's current wife, revealed the pistol in her hand. "I'm glad to see the little hit on the head I gave you didn't cause too much damage, Raleigh. There's still a lot we need to talk about since you shot the woman I sent to get me the information I needed from you."

Air evacuated from Raleigh's lungs as her fingers recalled the feel of pulling that trigger. She'd done it to save Beckett's life, just as she'd wielded that rock to save her brother's, but the blood was still on her hands. Always would be. "You hired Emily Cline to kill me."

"Yet here you are. Stubborn and determined as ever. I've always liked you. There was a point over the past few years I'd considered you a daughter, seeing as how Calvin and I never had children of our own, but you refused to play your part in my plan. Bringing Calvin's, or should I say Hank's, son into the investigation… Well, I couldn't have that. I've worked too hard and for too long to let you take this from me." Dark brown eyes settled on Calvin. Drywall debris skidded across the aged linoleum as Julia's muddied boots carved a path through the kitchen. Pink-tipped fingers smoothed over the gun in her left hand as Julia crouched beside her husband. "I lost count of how many times he'd tell me a story about Beckett, or his wife, or this place and how happy they'd been before she'd died. No matter how much I tried to be there for him, to be the wife he could be proud to have on his arm, I never came close to her, did I, Hank? Not once. Fifteen years of feeling unwanted, used, alone." Dejection surfaced as she rested the barrel of her gun over Calvin's heart. "Do you have any idea what that kind of pain does to a person?"

"You feel worthless. Underappreciated." Raleigh's throat dried as echoes of Beckett's accusations of conspiring against him and her own foundation pierced straight through her. Her heart pounded loud behind her ears. She knew what that kind of pain did to a person, what it'd done to her over the years. But what hurt more? Having it done by the one person in the world who'd convinced her she'd been valuable, who'd promised to always be there for her. For their daughter. Her voice hollowed as she retreated into the familiar sense of numbness she'd cultivated over the years. Only that space had shrunk over the past few days to the point she could barely get a grip. "You convince yourself there must be something wrong with you, that you're not worth being loved, and that there's no point in getting close to anyone because they're just going to discard you anyway. So you go numb to deal with the rejection, whether it's real or not, to feel like you have the slightest bit of control."

But it was a lie. Because there was always the chance someone would come along and rip that control away. As Beckett had done for her. He'd broken through her internal armor. He'd forced her to confront and question her deepest beliefs about herself, to feel things she'd closed herself off from for so long, and Raleigh feared she'd never be able to rebuild that wall. She didn't have the strength.

The weight of Julia Dailey's attention constrained the air in her lungs. A distance infused her voice, her expression smooth, and suddenly Raleigh had a vision of what her future looked like if she continued down this path. "Spoken like someone with firsthand experience. I think I'll be doing you a favor by putting you out of your misery sooner rather than later."

"Where is my son, Julia?" Calvin asked.

"You know, for a con man, you didn't do a very good job covering your tracks." Julia pushed to her feet. She studied the cracks in the walls, the single chair at the kitchen table, kicked at a stray root that'd worked through the flooring. "You've always talked about coming back here, renovating the property, working the land like you used to. You never told me the exact location, but it wasn't hard to find once I did a bit of digging through public records and put all the pieces together. Fitting this is going to be the place they find your body."

Calvin tried to lunge for his wife but came up short as the ropes held him back, and Raleigh pressed her lower back into the wall to counter the fear clawing through her. "Where is my son!"

"Don't worry, Hank. You'll be joining him very soon." Julia's low-pitched laugh filled the room. Her gaze flickered to Raleigh, her weapon still aimed at her husband. "Both of you will. Just as soon as Raleigh hands over my money."

Chapter Fourteen

Beckett parked the SUV about a quarter mile down the road from the ranch he'd grown up on and hit the headlights. Shadows closed in around him, and he shouldered out of the vehicle. Cool air mixed with dirt and the slight spice of trees as he rounded to the cargo area and popped the latch. Righting the storage container every deputy marshal under Remington Barton's purview was required to carry, he unhinged the lid and took what he needed. He strapped the extra Kevlar vest to his chest, the wound in his shoulder and side lighting up with a renewed edge of pain, and maneuvered the AK-15 strap over his neck. Extra mags and ammunition, a flashlight with fresh batteries and an additional handgun. Armed, he shut the case and secured the hatch.

His father had surprised him by hiring Emily Cline to do his dirty work, but the con man wouldn't see him coming this time. Neither would anyone who got in his way.

Keeping low, Beckett moved through the trees surrounding the property he hadn't ever expected to step foot on again. His boots suctioned in the mud with each step, the gear he carried getting heavier by the second, but he only pushed himself harder. Whoever'd opened fire on him and Raleigh had left the scene of the accident more than an hour ago. Hank had obviously needed Raleigh for something—maybe to access the secondary account she'd uncovered during her own investigation—but that didn't leave much time.

Twigs snapped under his weight as he circled closer to the fenced property line and crouched behind one of the largest pines to the west to get his bearings. He'd memorized every foot of this place and the surrounding woods when he'd been a kid, but a lot had changed since then. The stable roof had started caving in the middle, the wooden fence posts sagged toward one another and nature had overgrown the family cemetery less than fifty feet off to his left. The top of one tombstone—his mother's—stood out against the backdrop of night. Nobody had been here to take care of the land after he'd joined the Marshals, and for that he was sorry. He'd held the deed and paid the taxes all these years, but the thought of coming back here, of reliving that fearful night… It'd been too much.

Until now.

Beckett surveyed the shadows, focused on the slightest hint of movement near the main house.

There. At the southeast corner. His finger slipped alongside the trigger of the rifle he carried close to his chest as a single armed operative tossed a cigarette at his feet and ground out the ashes. Movement pulled Beckett's attention to the other side of the house. Another gunman, not quite as large as the first, but Beckett would assume just as deadly. Both his shoulder and thigh wounds burned in remembrance of the kind of violence Emily Cline had been capable of—of the type of people Hank had hired to keep his hands clean—and Beckett double-checked that the sonogram of his and Raleigh's baby was still in his pocket. He'd been trained in criminal apprehension for the past fifteen years, and nothing would stop him from getting to his fugitive. Raleigh was all he had left.

He hauled himself between the backer rails of the fence and took cover behind the west side of the stable. The second operative disappeared behind the house. Twenty feet separated him and his target. He had to move. Now. Back to the stable wall, he gripped the rifle between both hands and approached the far side. The odor of cigarette smoke and sweat burned the back of his throat, and Beckett pulled up short of rounding into the gunman's sights and raised his weapon. Hesitation pulsed through him. He couldn't take the shot. Not without tipping off the second operative and whoever Hank had inside with Raleigh. He couldn't force her abductors to panic and do something brash. Damn it.

Beckett repositioned the rifle at his back. His hands curled into fists.

He rushed forward. Beckett closed the distance between them fast, rocketing his fist into the side of the gunman's face. Bone crunched under his knuckles, but one shot didn't take the hired gun down. Clamping on to the operative's shoulder, he hiked his knee into the man's gut. The gunman blocked the hit with a groan, fisted Beckett's vest and threw him to the ground. The air crushed from his lungs a split second before a fist landed a hard right hook to his jaw.

Beckett's eyes watered as agony ripped through his head, but he managed to dodge the second hit aimed at his face and pushed to his feet. Dirt worked into his lungs as he wrapped the guard in his arms from behind and threw the man to the ground. Keeping hold of one wrist, he threaded the bastard's arm between his thighs and increased the pressure on the gunman's shoulder until a pop broke through their heavy breathing. A scream gurgled up the man's throat, and Beckett hauled the heel of his boot into the guy's head, knocking him unconscious.

"There goes the element of surprise." The gunman's scream had most likely given away his position. He unwound his legs from around the guard and got to his feet, but not fast enough.

The barrel of a pistol scratched the oversensitized skin along his scalp. "Drop the rifle, kick it away. Slowly. Along with any others you're carrying, Marshal Foster."

"You know me?" The muscles down his back hardened with battle-ready tension. The second operative. Damn it. Beckett turned his head enough to keep the gunman in his peripheral vision as he raised his palms shoulder height. He had no intention of giving up the rifle or any other weapons.

"I know enough." The second man tugged Beckett's backup weapon from his shoulder holster, along with the extra magazines he'd stocked on one side of his vest. A strong hand grasped Beckett's wounded shoulder and shoved him down before maneuvering the rifle strap over his head. "On your knees."

"If you say so." The pain flaring from the gunshot wound stole the oxygen from his chest but kicked his central nervous system into high gear. He'd come here to save Raleigh and his baby, and he wasn't leaving without them. Loose rocks ground into Beckett's knee as he turned around and shot both hands into the gunman's wrist and pushed upward. A gunshot arced wide before he pried the steel from his attacker's hand and tossed the weapon, but he couldn't let that slow him down. Straightening the shooter's arm, Beckett hauled his attacker into the side of his childhood farmhouse face-first.

The shooter wrenched his wrist out of Beckett's hold and swung a hard left hook. White lights raced across his vision as the hit threw him off-balance. He stumbled back, throwing his hands up to block the next hit, but his assailant was too fast. Another punch knocked his head straight back on his shoulders. Beckett struck out with a solid hit, but the gunman caught his fist and twisted until the muscles in his arm screamed. He shot his injured arm forward, connecting with the side of his attacker's head, but at the cost of tearing the stitches Reed had sewn in only recently. Undeniable agony tore through him, but he couldn't stop. Not until he'd found Raleigh.

The last rays of sun reflected off the gun he'd pried from the operative's grip, and Beckett lunged at the same time as his attacker. He wrapped his hands around the familiar weight of the weapon and shot to his feet before the mercenary had a chance to strike. Blood trickled down his arm beneath his shirt as he widened his stance and brought up the gun. "How many more of you did Hank hire? I need to know so I can be sure I have enough bullets when the time comes to shoot you."

"You've got it all wrong, Marshal." His attacker swiped at the blood from his mouth, spitting the excess at the ground. A low laugh penetrated through the ringing in his ear from the gun going off so close to his head. "You're not the one calling the shots here."

Multiple sets of footsteps echoed off the overhanging porch of the farmhouse. Another two operatives materialized on either side of him, two more at his back. He was outmanned and outgunned, and they knew it. Well, hell. He'd walked right into

Hank's trap, just as the bastard had probably intended from the beginning, and he'd been stupid enough—desperate enough—to follow along. Beckett shook his head, a laugh escaping past his mouth as he tossed the pistol in his hand into the dirt. "All right, then. Take me to the shot caller."

Two operatives flanked him from behind, one shoving him forward. His boots echoed off the old wood porch he'd spent so many summers running up and down as a kid. Hell, he could still see where his mother had recorded his height every year before school started on the front doorframe. The second gunman swung the porch screen wide and motioned him inside. As though Beckett had needed an invitation to walk inside his own damn house.

Peeling paint, splintered wood, rusted hinges. He ran his hand down along the corner of the doorframe. When this was over, when Hank was behind bars where he belonged and Beckett had cleared Raleigh's name of embezzling the money from the foundation, he'd come back here. He'd make this place the home his daughter deserved, somewhere Raleigh would feel safe. If she gave him the chance.

He crossed the threshold, the heaviness of mold and dust thick in his lungs. The outline of the brick fireplace demanded attention as they herded him through the main room toward the kitchen. Four operatives at his back, two outside. Not counting however many Hank had with him at all times. A man like that, who destroyed people's lives, was bound to have a few enemies. However, Beckett only had focus for the woman who'd had the guts to put a gun to Raleigh's head as he rounded into the small kitchen he used to know so well. The mother of his baby had been tied to an exposed length of plumbing. He shot forward, those captivating green eyes wide as the men behind him pulled him back. "Raleigh."

Pain exploded across the back of his head as one of the mercenaries at his back hit him from behind, and Beckett collapsed onto his knees. Raleigh's scream barely registered through the gag in her mouth, and the rage he'd become so familiar with over the years surged. Darkness closed in around the edges of his vision, but he had enough sense to make out the person holding the gun wasn't his father after all. That mistake went to Julia Dailey, Calvin Dailey's wife.

"I've never looked forward to family reunions, Marshal Foster," Julia said. "But I can't tell you how long I've been waiting to meet you."

He was bleeding.

Raleigh pulled at her restraints as one of the gunmen used the butt of his weapon to keep Beckett in line. He dropped to his knees, and her heart dropped with him. Her protest faded behind the piece of fabric Julia had shoved into her mouth when it became clear her men were under attack, and now the cause of that disruption was outnumbered and outgunned. One gunman pulled Beckett upright by the wound in his shoulder. Pain contorted his expression, and every cell in her body caught fire. She couldn't get to him, but one way or another, she'd make sure he got out of this alive.

"Perfect timing, Marshal. Ms. Wilde was about to transfer the money I've worked so hard to keep for myself back into my account." Julia increased the space between her and Raleigh, then swept the gun up. And took aim directly at Beckett. "That makes you the perfect motivation she needs to follow through."

"Glad I'm good for something other than a punching bag." Beckett swiped at his bloodied mouth, every bit the defensive, reliable marshal she'd fallen in love with over the past few days, and her insides clenched. "But you took something that belongs to me, so forgive me if I'm not in the family-reunion mood, ma'am."

Belonged to him? Did that mean...? Her heart shot into her throat.

He'd come here for her, to save her.

Her pulse throbbed at the base of her neck. Scouring the debris around her and Hank, Raleigh forced herself to focus on finding something— anything—that could cut through the ropes around her wrists. Desperation flooded into the tips of her fingers as she clawed at the thousands of threads making up her restraints. The second Julia forced her to log in to that account, Beckett would be out of time. They all would. She shifted her legs a few inches wider, and a soft scraping registered over the low drone of voices. A single piece of broken tile. Her mouth parted slightly. It must've broken off from the old countertop a few feet away. If she could somehow get it into her hands, she could cut through the ropes.

One look at Hank and she realized he'd made the same connection. He nodded. Blue eyes, not nearly as bright as his son's, shifted to Julia.

"Damn it, Julia, this is between you and me, and you've made your point." Hank struggled against the ropes, but it was no use. At least not without something to cut through them. "You were right. I never committed to you, even after we were married, and I'm sorry. I'm sorry I never gave you a fair chance. I'm sorry I never got over my wife. I'll blame myself for what happened to her every day for the rest of my life, and that guilt didn't leave much for anything else, especially you." Rough exhalations controlled the rise and fall of Hank's shoulders. "But you know as well as I do Raleigh and my son have nothing to do with this. They don't deserve to pay for the mistake I made. Please, let them go. I can get you the money. You and I can work this out. Together. We can start over."

Julia closed her eyes and lowered the weapon to her side, and Raleigh used the backs of her thighs to shift the piece of broken tile between her and Hank.

The woman's expression smoothed as the fight seemingly left her shoulders. "You have no idea how long I've been waiting to hear those words, Hank." She opened her eyes, and the muscles in Raleigh's legs seized. "But your apology is fifteen years too late."

Julia raised the gun and fired.

The bullet ripped into Hank's chest, and Raleigh couldn't hold back her muffled scream as blood splattered against one side of her face. Beckett cringed in his handlers' hold. The stain rapidly spread across Hank's white shirt, every second she couldn't stop the bleeding slipping through her fingers. Hank stared down at the wound as air hissed through his teeth, and he set his head back against the wall. "I just had this shirt cleaned."

"I underestimated you, Raleigh." Julia unpocketed a phone from her jumpsuit, the screen a bright beacon in the overcrowded kitchen, and handed it off to one of the men at her side. "You uncovered an account the FBI had no idea existed—my account—and drained everything I'd stolen from the foundation without me noticing, but you've always been impressive." She didn't so much as look at her husband as he bled out beside Raleigh, and a coldness worked through Raleigh's veins. Who was this woman? How hadn't Raleigh seen her for what she was until now? "Do you know how long it's taken me to plan this? I accounted for every step, every setback, for years before I put anything in motion, but I never expected you to run with my money."

The sun had gone down, intensifying the shadows along Beckett's jaw, the bruising and crusted blood darker than before. Confusion swirled through the crystal-blue eyes she hadn't been able to get out of her head for the past four months. "What the hell is she talking about? What did you do?"

"Go on, Raleigh. Tell him you're innocent, that he had you all wrong, and you fully intended to give the money you've taken from me back to the foundation where it belongs," Julia said. "Do you think he'll believe you this time, or does he already know the truth? That you're the one thing he hates most in this world. That you're exactly like his father."

Raleigh slid her attention to Beckett. He'd accused her of lying to him before, and he'd been partly right. Not about conspiring to steal all that money from the foundation with his father—or Julia—but because she'd stolen it back. Every dime. Emily Cline had set up the secondary account to funnel small increments without the FBI's notice at Julia's instruction, but she'd done it in Raleigh's name, with her personal information, to make the case against Raleigh stronger in case the feds caught on. Only that'd also given Raleigh access to the funds. Over one million dollars the FBI had no idea had been taken, a small percentage compared to the original fifty million that'd been stolen right out from under her nose. Her mouth dried as Beckett's expression hardened.

Julia reached out, soft skin sliding against Raleigh's cheek as she pulled the gag low. Hank struggled to breathe beside her but didn't warrant a single consideration from the woman who'd been married to him for fifteen years.

"I don't care where you moved it. I only want it back. Once I confirm the funds have been returned, you'll walk out of here alive. We can all move on with our lives and be happy in the knowledge that, after tonight, Hank and Beckett Foster won't ever be able to hurt us again." Julia stood. Centering the gun used to shoot her husband back on Beckett, she leveled her gaze on Raleigh. "Don't do as I ask, and I'll make it look like you killed the next man in the Foster lineup before his father bleeds out, which, from the looks of it, shouldn't be much longer. Is that what you want me to tell your daughter when she grows up, Raleigh? That her mother killed her father, a US marshal, and will spend the rest of her life behind bars?"

Nausea curdled in her stomach as Raleigh looked up at Julia. "What?"

"You didn't think I knew about the baby? I told you, Raleigh. I've planned for every setback of this plan. I'll be the only family she has left when this is all over, so getting custody won't be difficult when you're back in the FBI's possession." Julia had framed her for embezzling from the foundation she and Hank had built from the ground up. She'd hired mercenaries to keep her hands clean, shot her husband, who couldn't forgive himself for his past mistakes, and now the woman was threatening to kill the man Raleigh had stupidly fallen in love with and take her daughter from her. There was no way Julia would let them walk out of here alive. "Or you can put the money back where you found it and start your life over. Just you and your baby. Isn't that what you've always wanted? What you deserve?"

A predatorial growl registered a split second before Beckett shoved to his feet. He disarmed the gunman to his right and pulled the trigger. Once. Twice. Both men collapsed to the floor, and her marshal twisted around, putting Julia in his sights.

The nearest gunman cut the rope around Raleigh's wrists and wrenched her into his chest by her hair. In a matter of seconds, he pressed a long, cold blade against her throat. Hints of body odor rolled off his leather jacket, and Raleigh swallowed to counter the fear clawing through her. Two more guns for hire took position beside the door Beckett had come through, weapons trained on him. One wrong move, and she'd lose everything. "Beckett, no."

His gaze flickered to hers—cold, detached—and she lost feeling beneath her rib cage. She'd been wrong before. He'd tracked her back to his childhood ranch not because he'd realized he'd made a mistake accusing her of conspiracy or to prove he hadn't meant what he'd said. But because he was a US marshal assigned to recover his fugitive. Just as he'd always claimed.

"I've worked too hard for this. I deserve that money after what your father put me through," Julia said. "Shoot me, and you won't only lose him, Beckett. You'll lose your entire family."

"No, he won't." Fire simmered beneath the surface of Raleigh's skin. She closed her grip around the broken piece of tile she'd grabbed as the hit man with the knife had hauled her off the floor. Sharp stone cut into her palm, but the pain kept her grounded, focused, and Raleigh shot her elbow back into the gunman's gut. Following through with a knee to his face when he doubled over, she didn't bother watching him hit the floor as she turned on Julia. "Because we're not going any—"

Pain burned through her as Julia's gun discharged, and Raleigh froze. One second. Two. She followed the spread of blood across her shirt, so much closer to her navel than the piece of shrapnel from the car explosion. She stumbled back and touched the entry wound. Tears burned in her eyes before she tripped over one of Hank's feet and fell backward. She hit the floor, out of breath.

"No!" Beckett's yell reverberated through her, followed by three more gunshots.

She couldn't see him, couldn't move. She'd been

shot. Then silence. Strained breathing echoed around her after a few seconds, but she didn't have the strength to get up. "Beckett."

Chapter Fifteen

The rhythmic pulse of the machines recording her body's stats grated against the headache at the base of his skull. Three days. Raleigh should've come around from the anesthesia by now, but there wasn't any sign she intended to open her eyes and her doctors couldn't tell him anything more than he'd have to be patient. Things like this happened after experiencing the kind of trauma she'd been through.

Beckett leaned forward in the chair he'd set up beside her hospital bed. The surgeons had pulled the slug from her without any complications. He just needed her to wake up, and when she did, he'd be here. He wasn't going anywhere. Ever again.

He'd been such an idiot—for so many reasons, but more recently about the money she'd stolen from Julia Dailey, about conspiring with his father to steal from her own foundation. Raleigh hadn't taken those funds for her personal gain, as he'd feared. She could have. She could have run and never looked back, taken his daughter with her, and hell, he wouldn't have blamed her after what he'd done. But she hadn't. Instead, she'd proved once again to be a better person than he'd ever be, and she'd put them right back where they belonged.

In the foundation's accounts.

With Julia Dailey in federal custody, the FBI had had no other choice than to drop the accusations against Raleigh and close their investigation into the foundation. Beckett pressed his elbows against his knees and swiped his hand down his face. She was free, but at this rate, there was a chance he'd lose his fugitive all over again. The worst part was he'd brought it on himself.

Time had slowed when Julia had pulled that trigger. He'd watched the bullet leave the gun and race toward Raleigh. Only he hadn't been fast enough to stop it. With his entire future at risk, Beckett had turned his weapon on the two operatives behind him and left Julia Dailey to stand on her own. He'd secured his father's wife to the same pipe she'd tied Raleigh to as he'd waited for backup and the medical chopper, but every minute had felt like an hour.

A knock registered softly from behind, and Beckett swiped his hand down his face before standing to face the visitor. She hadn't had many over the past few days. Apart from him, the list mostly consisted of nurses, doctors and his team to update him on the investigation, but the last person he'd expected to set foot near the mother of his child darkened Raleigh's doorway.

Hank Foster.

"What the hell are you doing here?" Beckett stepped into the bastard responsible for this entire mess. If it hadn't been for his SOB father, for all the people he'd hurt, Raleigh wouldn't have been shot in the first place. She wouldn't have been targeted by Emily Cline or framed for stealing from the foundation. She wouldn't have been arrested and forced to go on the run to avoid their daughter growing up without her parents.

"I was discharged a couple hours ago, and one of the other marshals you work with told me you haven't left this room since Raleigh got out of surgery after he was done questioning me." Hank offered him a white foam box, eyes downcast. The man Beckett had spent twenty years of this life hating with every fiber of his being had the guts to look ashamed, apologetic. "I thought we could both use some real food, and I remembered you liked waffles, so I ordered some from that old diner we used to visit when you were a kid."

"Don't you dare say her name, Hank." The frustration, the anger, the desperation he'd been holding back since Beckett had stepped off the Life Flight chopper three days ago broke through the invisible dam he'd built in preparation for this moment. "You're the reason she's here. You're the reason your wife framed Raleigh and hired a hit woman to kill the best thing that's ever happened to me. No matter how far I've distanced myself from you,

from what you've done, I'm the one who's still paying the price for your mistakes. First with Mom,
now Raleigh. You put her in danger. You put my
baby in danger, and I'm not going to let you anywhere near either of them. Ever. Do you understand? I'm done with the past controlling my life,
dictating every decision I make, and I'm done with
you."

Hank retracted the box into his chest, the outline
of bandages clear between the unbuttoned section
of his shirt. "I'm sorry, Beckett. For everything.
Your mother was killed because of me. Because
of my selfishness. I was never arrested for what I
did, but I've spent the past twenty years working
to make that right, to be the father you deserve instead of the one you got. I don't know if it's possible given what's happened over the past few days,
but I'll spend another twenty years trying, if that's
what it takes. I'll keep the foundation going. I'll
help as many people as I can, and if you decide to
change your mind about where we go from here,
I'll be waiting." Hank nodded, and in that moment,
he suddenly looked older than a few minutes ago.
Setting the box of waffles on a nearby table, he
adjusted the suit jacket draped over his arm. "I'm
proud of you, son. You're going to be a great father
to that little girl, the kind she deserves."

"No thanks to you." Whether he'd said that more
for himself or to Hank, he didn't know. He didn't
care. Hank had apologized for what'd happened to

his mother, accepted responsibility for Julia's actions, but that wouldn't erase two decades' worth of hatred and anger. Their relationship—if they'd ever have one—would take more than a single conversation to heal, but at least he'd made his opinion on the matter clear.

"You've got one hell of a fighter on your hands, son, but if you want to be around much longer, eat the damn waffles. You look like you're going to fall over," Hank said.

The fight drained from Beckett as he turned back toward the bed and slid his hand in Raleigh's, but he could still feel Hank at the door. Fine. Beckett would let him see the damage he'd caused, how he'd almost destroyed the only family Beckett had left. He smoothed his thumb over her scabbed knuckles, and Raleigh's hand jerked in his. The hollowness under his rib cage intensified as his gaze shot to her face. "Raleigh?"

She squeezed her eyes shut, then opened them slowly. Hypnotic green eyes lifted to his, and relief flooded through him. Her chest collapsed on a strong exhalation as she shook her head. She licked dry lips, and he reached for the plastic mug provided by the hospital at the side of her bed. He set the straw against her mouth for her to take a drink, but her voice still graveled from the grogginess of being out cold for three days. "Beckett."

"I'm here. It's okay." Beckett kept her hand in his as he took his seat in the chair beside the bed.

"You were shot. Three days ago at the ranch. You were Life-Flighted here to the hospital in Portland where the surgeons were able to remove the bullet, but it took you a while to shake off the anesthesia."

"The baby." Panic infused her expression as she slid her free hand over her stomach above the sheets. Tears welled in her lower lash line, and she strengthened her grip on his hand. Raleigh fought to sit up straight, but the pain in her expression said her wound wouldn't let her get far. "Please tell me she's okay. Tell me the bullet didn't hurt—"

"She's fine." He brought her hand against his mouth, planting a kiss on the thin skin below her knuckles as he helped her settle back against the pillow. "Everything is fine. Julia Dailey was arrested, the charges against you were dropped, all of the missing donation funds have been returned to the foundation, and our daughter is exactly where she's supposed to be."

"Okay." She nodded, the distant haze in her eyes revealing she was still trying to get her bearings. After everything she'd been through, he wouldn't be surprised if it'd take her more than a few minutes to adjust. Hell, might even take months, and he intended to help her through it every step of the way. "I remember the gunshot, the blood on my shirt and that I couldn't see you after I fell. I thought I'd lost you both."

"You didn't lose anything. I'm here, she's here, and we're not going anywhere. It's over." Beckett worked small circles into the space between her index finger and thumb. His chest tightened at the fear still swirling in her gaze, and he repositioned her hand over his heart. He focused on the light blue veins running along the length of her arm. "Everything that happened was because of me. Julia wouldn't have gotten her hands on you in the first place if I hadn't let my own anger get in the way of seeing the truth, but when I saw who Calvin Dailey really was, that my father was part of this, I lost it, Raleigh."

Heat seared along his nerve endings at the memory, at the pain he'd put her through after he'd given his word to always be there for her. This woman had reached straight into his chest and claimed his heart, and he'd had no idea what he was supposed to do with that. Until now. "I couldn't see straight. I was fitting evidence into the puzzle that had nothing to do with the case, and I was scared. I've been disconnected for so damn long—living in the past—that I'd convinced myself I'd spend the rest of my days walking this earth alone, but then you came along. You kept me grounded even when I thought we wouldn't make it. You gave me purpose, and I was scared of losing that, of losing you and our baby. So I found a reason to make you the enemy to avoid having to feel that pain ever again. I was stupid for considering you'd been involved with Hank's next con, and I'm sorry. I'm sorry for breaking my word to always be there for you when you deserved so much better. I can't promise I won't be an idiot in the future, but I sure as hell won't ever doubt you again. If you'll just give me the chance to prove it."

She tugged her hand from his and set it over her slight baby bump. The muscles in her throat worked to swallow. She kept her expression neutral as she raised her gaze to his. The answer was so clear in those beautiful green eyes, the pain he'd caused evident, and his gut soured. "I don't know if that's possible anymore. I haven't felt important to anyone my whole life, Beckett. Everyone I've let get close has walked away once I didn't serve a purpose for them anymore, but when we were in that cabin, you made me feel like I could've been important. That you saw me just for me and not something to be used." She tilted her head to one side, tears sliding down her cheeks. "I was falling in love with you, dreaming about waking up next to you every morning on that ranch the marshals seized, taking family trips into town, teaching our daughter how to ride her first horse. It felt so real. I wanted it to be real." Her voice hollowed. "But I realized it'd been a fantasy. All of it. Because until you recognize you have people who want to be there for you—that you're the one who's been pushing them away—there isn't going to be room in your life for me or for our daughter."

His throat threatened to swell shut. "What are… what are you saying?"

"I'm saying we're always going to be connected

because of this baby. There's no denying that," she said, "but I'm going to let the lawyers handle everything from here."

SHE SHOULDN'T BE HERE.

Raleigh stepped out of the old four-door sedan she'd purchased a few days after being released from the hospital. Her car, her apartment, her belongings, it'd all been taken by the state once she'd been arrested, but that was behind her now. It was time to start over, fresh, but she hadn't planned on ever coming back here.

Her past had been burned clean, and she was going to take advantage. If it hadn't been at Beckett's insistence they meet here to review the paternity and custody papers before their lawyers submitted them to the courts, she never would've driven out here. She'd made it clear in the hospital she'd hand off any legal matters concerning their daughter to her lawyer, negating any reason for them to have to see each other until the baby was born, but he'd sounded desperate over the phone. Broken.

She couldn't deny she was hurting just as badly at what'd happened between them.

She breathed in the slight hint of pines and hay for a few moments. Yellowing grass swayed in the breeze as she followed the dirt road leading to the main farmhouse. The seized property looked the same as it had a few weeks ago—when Emily Cline had caught up with them—but where fear had controlled her then, beauty met her now. She burrowed into her coat as the large barn at the edge of the property demanded her attention before she stepped onto the house's pale front porch. She lifted her hand to knock before the door swung inward.

And there he was.

A tingling sensation bubbled inside her as his gaze studied her from head to toe. His beard seemed thicker, the lines around his eyes and mouth a little deeper as though he hadn't slept in a while, and her heart hiccuped in her chest. It'd been only two weeks since she'd woken to find him next to her hospital bed, but so much had changed since then. Those brilliant blue eyes brightened, and she fought the rush of need she'd been working to bury as it seeped through the cracks in her shattered armor. He was handsome as ever with the white long-sleeved shirt, jeans, boots and no visible signs of his blood or anyone else's staining his clothes, and it took her a few breaths to remember why she was here. "I didn't think you'd come out here."

"You wanted me to double-check the paperwork before we go to court." Raleigh folded her arms across her chest. The siding beside the door smelled of fresh paint the longer she stood there, but there was no reason the US Marshals would be fixing the place up unless they were getting it ready for public auction. A strange heaviness settled in her gut at the thought. For the past few weeks she'd been staying in a hotel room while the FBI concluded their investigation, but soon she'd have to find a more permanent place. She and Beckett had almost been killed right near here, but that didn't detract from the sense of peace—of home—she'd experienced before the gunwoman had fired that first bullet. "If we're going to make this coparenting thing work, we're each going to have to make an effort. This is mine."

"I appreciate it." He shifted back on his heels, motioning her through the door. "Come in."

She stepped over the threshold, that immediate feeling of calm washing over her. Warmth flooded over the exposed skin of her neck and hands from the fireplace as she took in the wall of windows and pale gray-and-white decor. Everything looked the same, felt the same. Only they weren't. Not with Beckett.

He'd taken responsibility for his mistake in accusing her of conspiracy, in arresting her mere hours after promising to always be there. His admission of letting the anger he'd held on to all these years get in the way of his judgment still echoed in her head when she lay alone at night. He'd asked for another chance, and she'd been so tempted to give it, to forget he'd turned his back on her all over again. But she couldn't.

Because what would stop him from turning his back on her the next time? What would stop him from leaving her as an only parent when all that anger clouded his judgment again?

In that moment, Raleigh had imagined having to explain to their baby girl why her father had disappeared. She'd seen the disappointment in her daughter's eyes so clearly, experienced that feeling of being unwanted by the man she'd look up to, heard their child convincing herself she wasn't worth loving. That single image had broken what was left of Raleigh's heart in a matter of seconds, but she had the power to make sure it never became reality. By coparenting with Beckett as agreed, but nothing more. No commitment. No emotions. Nothing that he could use to hurt her or their daughter down the line.

Closing the door behind her, Beckett moved ahead of her deeper into the house. His boots echoed off the dark hardwood flooring, each step a physical and invisible wedge between them. "I've got the documents in the kitchen and some snacks if you need. I know it's a long drive, and I'm guessing you probably didn't think to pack anything to eat before you left."

"I didn't." She followed him into the kitchen and ran her fingers across the cold white granite of the kitchen island as he rounded behind it. A stack of documents and pens had been positioned on one side, along with a couple of bottled waters and an assortment of fresh fruit. The weight of his attention constricted the air in her lungs. She reached for the papers. "You could've emailed me the documents. We didn't have to meet all the way out here."

"The papers aren't the only thing I wanted to have you look over." Beckett came around the island, every muscle across his chest and along his shoulders flexing and releasing with each step, and her skin prickled with his proximity. A combination of pine and hard work dived into her lungs as he slid something across the granite. The scrape of metal jarred her back from the edge of leaning into him.

Keys? Raleigh pinched the metal ring between her index finger and thumb, studying them as though she'd be able to recognize them at a glance. "What are these for?"

"This place." Beckett pressed his palms onto the stone as he leveled that blue gaze on her. "It's yours."

What? Her throat got tight. "I'm sorry. I think my brain left my body there for a second. Can you repeat that?"

"In the hospital you told me you'd imagined waking up here every day, of teaching our daughter to ride, that it'd all felt real when you were here. So I bought the property back from the Marshals Service before it could go to public auction, and I'm giving it to you. These papers aren't for custody of our daughter. They're to sign the deed to this place over to you." He stepped into her, unbearably close, which forced her to look up at him, and she suddenly didn't have the mind to confirm what the papers said.

She only had attention for him. For all that dark

hair she'd run her fingers through a dozen times, for the strong tendons between his neck and shoulders she'd held on to when they'd been on the run for their lives, for the softness of his mouth when he'd kissed her. She planted her hand against his chest, her head urging her to push him away, to regain her composure, but the familiar beat of his heart under her palm reverberated through her.

He'd bought her the ranch?

"I know why you wanted the lawyers involved, and you had every reason to get as far from me as you could these past couple of weeks. Seeing how this anger I've carried around has hurt you and any chance I have at being a father to that baby girl brought me to the lowest point of my life." He lowered his gaze to her hands as he took them both in his. "I've been hanging on to it as a crutch for so long, I wasn't sure I could get by if I had to let it go, but you leaving made me realize I wanted you more than I wanted to hate Hank. I'm not sure I'll ever be able to forgive him for what he's done, but I'm willing to try. For you. For our baby."

He smoothed calming circles into the backs of her hands, and she was overtaken by need. By the feeling of complete and utter destruction she'd been trying to ignore since she'd been discharged from the hospital. "I can't take another second being apart from you. I can't live the rest of my life handing off our daughter at neutral locations or only seeing you for a few minutes at a time every couple of weeks. I can't pretend I'm okay with the thought of you finding someone else or being with anyone other than me. I can't. I'm in love with you, Raleigh, and I want to work to make you and our daughter happy for the rest of our lives. And that means I'm not going anywhere. Ever."

He released her and dropped to one knee.

"What are you doing?" She slid her hand over her stomach, waiting for reassurance as she'd done a hundred times over the past few months, but she couldn't think straight. Couldn't breathe. He'd bought her a ranch to show he loved her. She'd gotten so used to people walking away over the years, to pretending their actions hadn't hurt, but the truth was Beckett had cut deeper than them all. He'd cut through her sense of worthlessness, her feeling of being unwanted by everyone around her, cut through the numbness she was comfortable living with the rest of her life. Where others had left her empty and exhausted, he'd made her whole and given her a gift no one else had ever before: hope for the future.

"Raleigh Wilde, I love you." Beckett pulled a small black box from his front pocket and flipped it open. In the center of lush cream silk was a simple solitaire embedded in a thick band, and the connection she'd relied on during those terrifying few days of their secret investigation flooded through her. "Will you marry me?"

"Yes." She fell into him and wrapped her arms around his neck as she straddled him right there in the middle of the kitchen floor. Her kitchen floor. He held on to her, and everything she'd ever wanted came within reach. A stable home, a partner who had her back, a family. It was all hers. Raleigh slid her mouth over his, her heart threatening to beat straight out of her chest. "I love you, too, but the next time you feel the need to arrest me, you better be ready for the fight of your life."

Beckett wrapped her in the circle of his arms. "The next time I feel the need to arrest you, I promise to give you a head start."

* * * * *

*When K-9 handler Serena Lopez discovers her half
brother's a fugitive from justice, she must find him—and his
dangerous crew. It's a good thing her partner is lead agent
Axel Morrow. But as cunning as the duo may be, it's a race
against time to catch the criminals before they kill again.*

Read on for a sneak preview of
Hunting a Killer *by Nicole Helm.*

Prologue

The tears leaked out of Kay Duvall's eyes, even as she tried to
focus on what she had to do. *Had* to do to bring Ben home safe.

She fumbled with her ID and punched in the code that
would open the side door, usually only used for a guard taking a
smoke break. It would be easy for the men behind her to escape
from this side of the prison.

It went against everything she was supposed to do.
Everything she considered right and good.

A quiet sob escaped her lips. They had her son. How could
she not help them escape? Nothing mattered beyond her son's
life.

"Would you stop already?" one of the prisoners muttered.
He'd made her give him her gun, which he now jabbed into her
back. "Crying isn't going to change anything. So just shut up."

She didn't care so much about her own life or if she'd be
fired. She didn't care what happened to her as long as they let
her son go. So she swallowed down the sobs and blinked out as
many tears as she could, hoping to stem the tide of them.

She got the door open and slid out first—because the man holding the gun pushed it into her back until she moved forward.

They came through the door behind her, dressed in the clothes she'd stolen from the locker room and Lost and Found. Anything warm she could get her hands on to help them escape into the frigid February night.

Help them escape. Help three dangerous men escape prison. When she was supposed to keep them inside.

It didn't matter anymore. She just wanted them gone. If they were gone, they'd let her baby go. They had to let her baby go.

Kay forced her legs to move, one foot in front of the other, toward the gate she could unlock without setting off any alarms. She unlocked it, steadier this time if only because she kept thinking that once they were gone, she could get in contact with Ben.

She flung open the gate and gestured them out into the parking lot. "Stay out of the safety lights and no one should bug you."

"You better hope not," one of the men growled.

"The minute you sound that alarm, your kid is dead. You got it?" This one was the ringleader. The one who'd been in for murder. Who else would he kill out there in the world?

Guilt pooled in Kay's belly, but she had to ignore it. She had to live with it. Whatever guilt she felt would be survivable. Living without her son wouldn't be. Besides, she had to believe they'd be caught. They'd do something else terrible and be caught.

As long as her son was alive, she didn't care.

Don't miss
Hunting a Killer *by Nicole Helm,*
available February 2021 wherever
Harlequin Intrigue books and ebooks are sold.

Harlequin.com

HIEXP0121

Love Harlequin romance?

DISCOVER.

Be the first to find out about promotions,
news and exclusive content!

 Facebook.com/HarlequinBooks

Twitter.com/HarlequinBooks

Instagram.com/HarlequinBooks

Pinterest.com/HarlequinBooks

ReaderService.com

EXPLORE.

Sign up for the Harlequin e-newsletter and
download a free book from any series at
TryHarlequin.com

CONNECT.

Join our Harlequin community to
share your thoughts and connect
with other romance readers!
Facebook.com/groups/HarlequinConnection

HSOCIAL2020